Mr Mu
Ghosts

Mr Mukerji's Ghosts

Supernatural Tales from the
British Raj Period
by India's Ghost Story 'Collector'

S. Mukerji

LEONAUR

Mr Mukerji's Ghosts: Supernatural Tales from the British Raj Period by India's Ghost Story 'Collector'
by S. Mukerji

Originally published in 1917 under the title
Indian Ghost Stories

Published by Leonaur Ltd

Text in this form copyright © 2006 Leonaur Ltd

ISBN (10 digit): 1-84677-102-1 (hardcover)
ISBN (13 digit): 978-1-84677-102-6 (hardcover)

ISBN (10 digit): 1-84677-093-9 (softcover)
ISBN (13 digit): 978-1-84677-093-7 (softcover)

http://www.leonaur.com

Publisher's Notes

In the interests of authenticity, the spellings, grammar and place names used have been retained from the original editions.

The opinions of the authors represent a view of events in which he was a participant related from his own perspective, as such the text is relevant as an historical document.

The views expressed in this book are not necessarily those of the publisher.

Contents

From the Desk of S. Mukerji Esq.	7
His Dead Wife's Photograph	10
The Major's Lease	17
The Disembodied Hand	26
The Leaping Woman	31
The Open Door	32
The Sleeper	38
What Uncle Saw	42
The Weekend Wife	47
The Boy Who Was Caught	52
Two Ghosts	57
The Haunted Well	62
The Strange Tree	66
The Starving Millionaire	68
The Black Artist	80
The Bridal Party	87
The Governor General's House	93
Open Windows	95
You Will Like to Kiss It	97
The Haunted Tank	101
A Strange Incident	104
A Suttee Story	109
The Return of Smith	112
What the Professor Saw	118
The Astral Lady & Others	122

On the Train & Others	127
The Boy Possessed	132
The Burning	138
The Examination Paper	143
The Shakespeare Expert	147
The Messenger of Death	151
Goats	153
The Messenger of Death II	156
From the Desk of S. Mukerji Esq.	161
The White Lady of the Hohenzollerns	163

FROM THE DESK OF:
S. Mukerji Esq.,
Ghost Story Collector Extraordinary
Calcutta

July 1914

Dear Honoured and Esteemed Reader

I do not know whether writing ghost stories is a mistake.

Most readers will like a ghost story in which towards the end it is found that the ghost was really a cat or a dog or a mischievous boy.

Such ghost stories are a source of pleasure, and are read as a pastime and are often vastly enjoyed, because though the reader is a bit afraid of what he does not know, still he likes to be assured that ghosts do not in reality exist.

Such ghost stories I have often myself read and enjoyed. The last one I read was in the December (1913) Number of the *English Illustrated Magazine*. In that story coincidence follows coincidence in such beautiful succession that a young lady really believes that she sees a ghost and even feels its touch, and finally it turns out that it is only a monkey.

This is bathos that unfortunately goes too far. Still, I am sure, English readers love a ghost story of this kind.

It, however, cannot be denied that particular incidents do sometimes happen in such a way that they take our breath away. Here is something to the point.

"Twenty years ago, near Honey Grove, in Texas, James Ziegland, a wealthy young farmer won the hand of Metilda Tichnor, but jilted her a few days before the day fixed for the marriage. The girl, a celebrated beauty, became despondent and killed herself. Her brother, Phil, went to James Ziegland's home and after denouncing him, fired at him. The bullet grazed the cheek of the faithless lover and buried itself in a tree. Young Tichnor, supposing he had killed the man, put a bullet into his own head, dying instantly. Ziegland, subsequently married a wealthy widow. All this was, of course 20 years ago. The other day the farmer James Ziegland and his son cut down the tree in which Tichnor's bullet had lodged. The tree proved too tough for splitting and so a small charge of dynamite was used. The explosion discharged the long forgotten bullet with great force, it pierced Ziegland's head and he fell mortally wounded. He explained the existence of the mysterious bullet as he lay on his deathbed."

—*The Pioneer, Allahabad*, (India,) 31st January, 1913.

In India ghosts and their stories are looked upon with respect and fear. I have heard all sorts of ghost stories from my nurse and my father's coachman, Abdullah, who used to be my constant companion in my childhood, (dear friend, who is no more), as well as from my friends who are Judges and Magistrates and other responsible servants of Government, and in two cases from Judges of Indian High Courts.

A story told by a nurse or a coachman should certainly

not be reproduced in this book. In this book, there are a few of those stories only which are true to the best of the author's knowledge and belief.

Some of these narratives may, no doubt, savour too much of the nature of a cock and bull story, but the reader must remember that "there are more things in heaven and earth, etc." and that truth is sometimes stranger than fiction.

The author is responsible for the arrangement of the stories in this volume. Probably they could have been better arranged; but a little thought will make it clear why this particular sequence has been selected.

S. Mukerji

His Dead Wife's Photograph

> This story created a sensation when it was first told. It appeared in the papers and many big Physicists and Natural Philosophers were, at least so they thought, able to explain the phenomenon. I shall narrate the event and also tell the reader what explanation was given, and let him draw his own conclusions. This was what happened.

A friend of mine, a clerk in the same office as myself, was an amateur photographer; let us call him Jones.

Jones had a half plate Sanderson camera with a Ross lens and a Thornton Picard behind lens shutter, with pneumatic release. The plate in question was a Wrattens ordinary, developed with Ilford Pyro Soda developer prepared at home. All these particulars I give for the benefit of the more technical reader.

Mr. Smith, another clerk in our office, invited Mr. Jones to take a likeness of his wife and sister-in-law.

This sister-in-law was the wife of Mr. Smith's elder brother, who was also a Government servant, then on leave. The idea of the photograph was of the sister-in-law.

Jones was a keen photographer himself. He had photographed every body in the office including the peons and sweepers, and had even supplied every sitter of his with copies of his handiwork. So he most willingly consented, and anxiously waited for the Sunday on which the photograph was to be taken.

Early on Sunday morning, Jones went to the Smiths'. The arrangement of light in the verandah was such that a photograph could only be taken after midday; and so he stayed there to breakfast.

At about one in the afternoon all arrangements were complete and the two ladies, Mrs. Smiths, were made to sit in two cane chairs and after long and careful focussing, and moving the camera about for an hour, Jones was satisfied at last and an exposure was made. Mr. Jones was sure that the plate was all right; and so, a second plate was not exposed although in the usual course of things this should have been done.

He wrapped up his things and went home promising to develop the plate the same night and bring a copy of the photograph the next day to the office.

The next day, which was a Monday, Jones came to the office very early, and I was the first person to meet him.

"Well, Mr. Photographer," I asked "what success?"

"I got the picture all right," said Jones, unwrapping an unmounted picture and handing it over to me "most funny, don't you think so?"

"No, I don't... I think it is all right, at any rate I did not expect anything better from you...", I said.

"No," said Jones "the funny thing is that only two ladies sat..."

"Quite right," I said "the third stood in the middle."

"There was no third lady at all there...", said Jones.

"Then you imagined she was there, and there we find her..."

"I tell you, there were only two ladies there when I exposed" insisted Jones. He was looking awfully worried.

"Do you want me to believe that there were only two persons when the plate was exposed and three when it was developed?" I asked.

"That is exactly what has happened," said Jones.

"Then it must be the most wonderful developer you used, or was it that this was the second exposure given to the same plate?"

"The developer is the one which I have been using for the last three years, and the plate, the one I charged on Saturday night out of a new box that I had purchased only on Saturday afternoon."

A number of other clerks had come up in the meantime, and were taking great interest in the picture and in Jones' statement.

It is only right that a description of the picture be given here for the benefit of the reader. I wish I could reproduce the original picture too, but that for certain reasons is impossible.

When the plate was actually exposed there were only two ladies, both of whom were sitting in cane chairs. When the plate was developed it was found that there was in the picture a figure, that of a lady, standing in the middle. She wore a broad-edged dhoti (the reader should not forget that all the characters are Indians), only the upper half of her body being visible, the lower being covered up by the low backs of the cane chairs. She was distinctly behind the chairs, and consequently slightly out of focus. Still everything was quite clear. Even her long necklace was visible through the little opening in the dhoti near the right shoulder. She was resting her hands on the backs of the chairs and the fingers were nearly totally out of focus, but a ring on the right ring-finger was clearly visible. She looked like a handsome young woman of twenty-two, short and thin. One of the ear-rings was also clearly visible, although the face itself was slightly out of focus. One thing, and probably the funniest thing, that we overlooked then but observed afterwards, was that immediately behind the three ladies was a barred window. The two ladies, who were one on each side, covered up the bars to a certain height from the bottom with their bodies, but the lady in the middle was partly transparent because the bars of the window were very faintly visible through her. This fact, however, as I have said already, we did not observe then. We only laughed at Jones and tried to assure him that he was either drunk or asleep. At this moment Smith of our office walked in, removing the trouser clips from his legs.

Smith took the unmounted photograph, looked at it for a minute, turned red and blue and green and finally very pale. Of course, we asked him what the matter was and this was what he said:

"The third lady in the middle was my first wife, who has been dead these eight years. Before her death she asked me a number of times to have her photograph taken. She used to say that she had a presentiment that she might die early. I did not believe in her presentiment myself, but I did not object to the photograph. So one day I ordered the carriage and asked her to dress up. We intended to go to a good professional. She dressed up and the carriage was ready, but as we were going to start news reached us that her mother was dangerously ill. So we went to see her mother instead. The mother was very ill, and I had to leave her there. Immediately afterwards I was sent away on duty to another station and so could not bring her back. It was in fact after full three months and a half that I returned and then though her mother was all right, my wife was not. Within fifteen days of my return she died of puerperal fever after child-birth and the child died too. A photograph of her was never taken. When she dressed up for the last time on the day that she left my home she had the necklace and the ear-rings on, as you see her wearing in the photograph. My present wife has them now but she does not generally put them on."

This was too big a pill for me to swallow. So I at once took French leave from my office, bagged the photograph and rushed out on my bicycle. I went to Mr. Smith's house and looked Mrs. Smith up. Of course, she was much astonished to see a third lady in the picture but could not guess who she was. This I had expected, as supposing Smith's story to be true, this lady had never seen her husband's first wife. The elder brother's wife, however, recognized the likeness at once and she virtually repeated the story which Smith had told me earlier that day. She even brought out the necklace and the ear-rings for my inspection and conviction. They were the same as those in the photograph.

All the principal newspapers of that time got hold of the fact and within a week there was any number of applications for the ghostly photograph. But Mr. Jones refused to supply copies of it to anybody for various reasons, the principal being that Smith would not allow it. I am, however, the fortunate possessor of a copy which, for obvious reasons, I am not allowed to show to anybody. One copy of the picture was sent to America and another to England. I do not now remember exactly to whom. My own copy I showed to the Rev. Father——M.A., D.SC., B.D., etc., and asked him to find out a scientific explanation of the phenomenon. The following explanation was given by the gentleman. (I am afraid I shall not be able to reproduce the learned Father's exact words, but this is what he meant or at least what I understood him to mean).

"The girl in question was dressed in this particular way on an occasion, say 10 years ago. Her image was cast on space and the reflection was projected from one luminous body (one planet) on another till it made a circuit of millions and millions of miles in space and then came back to earth at the exact moment when our friend, Mr. Jones, was going to make the exposure.

"Take for instance the case of a man who is taking the photograph of a mirage. He is photographing place X from place Y, when X and Y are, say, 200 miles apart, and it may be that his camera is facing east while place X is actually towards the west of place Y."

In school I had read a little of Science and Chemistry and could make a dry analysis of a salt; but this was an item too big for my limited comprehension.

The fact, however, remains and I believe it, that Smith's first wife did come back to this terrestrial globe of ours over eight years after her death to give a sitting for a photograph in a form which, though it did not affect the retina of our eye, did impress a sensitized plate; in a form that did not affect the retina of the eye, I say, because Jones must have been looking at his sitters at the time when he was pressing the bulb of the pneumatic release of his time and instantaneous shutter.

The story is most wonderful but this is exactly what happened. Smith says this is the first time he has ever seen, or heard from, his dead wife. It is popularly believed in India that a dead wife gives a lot of trouble, if she ever revisits this earth, but this is, thank God, not the experience of my friend, Mr. Smith.

It is now over seven years since the event mentioned above happened; and the dead girl has never appeared again. I would very much like to have a photograph of the two ladies taken once more; but I have never ventured to approach Smith with the proposal. In fact, I learnt photography myself with a view to take the photograph of the two ladies, but as I have said, I have never been able to speak to Smith about my intention, and probably never shall. The £10, that I spent on my cheap photographic outfit may be a waste. But I have learnt an art which though rather costly for my limited means is nevertheless an art worth learning.

The Major's Lease

A curious little story was told the other day in a certain Civil Court in British India.

A certain military officer, let us call him Major Brown, rented a house in one of the big Cantonment stations where he had been recently transferred with his regiment.

This gentleman had just arrived from England with his wife. He was the son of a rich man at home and so he could afford to have a large house. This was the first time he had come out to India and was consequently rather unacquainted with the manners and customs of this country.

Major Brown took this house on a long lease and thought he had made a bargain. The house was large and stood in the centre of a very spacious compound. There was a garden which appeared to have been carefully laid out once, but as the house had no tenant for a long time the garden looked more like a wilderness. There were two very well kept lawn tennis courts and these were a great attraction to the Major, who was very keen on tennis. The stablings and out-houses were commodious and the Major, who was thinking of keeping a few polo ponies, found the whole thing very satisfactory. Over and above everything he found the landlord very obliging. He had heard on board the steamer on his way out that Indian landlords were the worst class of human beings one could come across on the face of this earth (and that is very true), but this particular landlord looked like an exception to the general rule.

He consented to make at his own expense all the alterations that the Major wanted him to do, and these alterations were carried out to Major and Mrs. Brown's entire satisfaction.

On his arrival in this station Major Brown had put up at an hotel and after some alterations had been made he ordered the house to be furnished. This was done in three or four days and then he moved in.

Annexed is a rough sketch of the house in question. The house was a very large one and there was a number of rooms, but we have nothing to do with all of them. The spots marked "C" and "E" represent the doors.

Now what happened in Court was this:

After he had occupied the house for not over three weeks the Major and his wife cleared out and took shelter again in the hotel from which they had come. The landlord demanded rent for the entire period stipulated for in the lease and the Major refused to pay. The matter went to Court. The presiding Judge, who was an Indian gentleman, was one of the cleverest men in the service, and he thought it was a very simple case.

When the case was called on the plaintiff's pleader said that he would begin by proving the lease. Major Brown, the defendant, who appeared in person, said that he would admit it. The Judge who was a very kind hearted gentleman asked the defendant why he had vacated the house.

"I could not stay," said the Major "I had every intention of living in the house, I got it furnished and spent two thousand rupees over it, I was laying out a garden...."

The Major's Lease

"But what do you mean by saying that you could not stay?"

"If your Honour passed a night in that house, you would understand what I meant," said the Major.

"You take the oath and make a statement," said the Judge. Major Brown then made the following statement on oath in open Court.

"When I came to the station I saw the house and my wife liked it. We asked the landlord whether he would make a few alterations and he consented. After the alterations had been carried out I executed the lease and ordered the house to be furnished. A week after the execution of the lease we moved in. The house is very large."

Here followed a description of the building; but to make matters clear and short I have copied out the rough pencil sketch which is still on the record of the case and marked the doors and rooms, as the Major had done, with letters.

"I do not dine at the mess. I have an early dinner at home with my wife and retire early. My wife and I sleep in the same bedroom (the room marked "G" in the plan), and we are generally in bed at about 11 o'clock at night. The servants all go away to the out-houses which are at a distance of about 40 yards from the main building, only one Jamadar (porter) remains in the front verandah. This Jamadar also keeps an eye on the whole main building, besides I have got a good, faithful watch dog which I brought out from home. He stays outside with the Jamadar.

"For the first fifteen days we were quite comfortable, then the trouble began.

"One night before dinner my wife was reading a story, a detective story, of a particularly interesting nature. There were only a few more pages left and so we thought that she would finish them before we put out the reading lamp. We were in the bedroom. But it took her much longer than she had expected it would, and so it was actually half an hour after midnight when we put out the big sixteen candle power reading lamp which stood on a teapoy near the head of the beds. Only a small bedroom lamp remained.

"But though we put out the light we did not fall asleep. We were discussing the cleverness of the detective and the folly of the thief who had left a clue behind, and it was actually two o'clock when we pulled our rugs up to our necks and closed our eyes.

"At that moment we heard the footsteps of a number of persons walking along the corridor. The corridor runs the whole length of the house as will appear from the rough sketch. This corridor was well carpeted still we heard the tread of a number of feet. We looked at the door "C." This door was closed but not bolted from inside. Slowly it was pushed open, and, horror of horrors, three shadowy forms walked into the room. One was distinctly the form of a white man in European night attire, another the form of a white woman, also in night attire, and the third was the form of a black woman, probably an Indian nurse or ayah.

"We remained dumb with horror, as we could see clearly that these unwelcome visitors were not of this world. We could not move.

"The three figures passed right round the beds as if searching for something. They looked into every nook and corner of the bed-room and then passed into the dressing room. Within half a minute they returned and passed out into the corridor in the same order in which they had come in, namely, the man first, the white woman next, and the black woman last of all.

"We lay as if dead. We could hear them in the corridor and in the bedroom adjoining, with the door "E", and in the dressing room attached to that bedroom. They again returned and passed into the corridor... and then we could hear them no more.

"It must have taken me at least five minutes to collect my senses and to bring my limbs under control. When I got up I found that my wife had fainted. I hurried out of the room, rushed along the corridor, opened the front door and called the servants. The servants were all approaching the house across the land which separated the servants' quarters from the main building. Then I went into the dining room, and procuring some brandy, gave it to my wife. It was with some difficulty that I could make her swallow it, but it revived her and she looked at me with a bewildered smile on her face.

"The servants had in the meantime arrived and were in the corridor. Their presence had the effect of giving us some courage. Leaving my wife in bed I went out and related to the servants what I had seen. The Chaukidar (the night watchman) who was an old resident of the compound (in fact he had been in charge of the house when it was vacant, before I rented it) gave me the history of the ghost, which my Jamadar interpreted to me. I have brought the Chaukidar and shall produce him as my witness."

This was the statement of the Major. Then there was the statement of Jokhi Passi, Chaukidar, defendant's witness.

The statement of this witness as recorded was as follows:

> "My age is 60 years. At the time of the Indian Mutiny I was a full-grown young man. This house was built at that time. I mean two or three

years after the Mutiny. I have always been in charge. After the Mutiny one Judge came to live in the house. He was called Judge Parson (probably Pearson). The Judge had to try a young Muhammadan charged with murder and he sentenced the youth to death. The aged parents of the young man vowed vengeance against the good Judge. On the night following the morning on which the execution took place it appeared that certain undesirable characters were prowling about the compound. I was then the watchman in charge as I am now. I woke up the Indian nurse who slept with the Judge's baby in a bed-room adjoining the one in which the Judge himself slept. On waking up she found that the baby was not in its cot. She rushed out of the bed-room and informed the Judge and his wife. Then a feverish search began for the baby, but it was never found. The police were communicated with and they arrived at about four in the morning. The police enquiry lasted for about half an hour and then the officers went away promising to come again. At last the Judge, his wife, and nurse all retired to their respective beds where they were found lying dead later in the morning. Another police enquiry took place, and it was found that death was due to snake-bite. There were two small punctures on one of the legs of each victim. How a snake got in and killed each victim in turn, especially when two slept in one room and the third in another, and finally got out, has remained a mystery. But the

Judge, his wife, and the nurse are still seen on every Friday night looking for the missing baby. One rainy season the servants' quarters were being re-roofed. I had then an occasion to sleep in the corridor; and thus I saw the ghosts. At that time I was as afraid as the Major Saheb is to-day, but then I soon found out that the ghosts were quite harmless."

This was the story as recorded in Court. The Judge was a very sensible man (I had the pleasure and honour of being introduced to him about 20 years after this incident), and with a number of people, he decided to pass one Friday night in the haunted house. He did so. What he saw does not appear from the record; for he left no inspection notes and probably he never made any. He delivered judgment on Monday following. It is a very short judgment.

After reciting the facts the judgment proceeds:

"I have recorded the statements of the defendant and a witness produced by him. I have also made a local inspection. I find that the landlord, (the plaintiff) knew that for certain reasons the house was practically uninhabitable, and he concealed that fact from his tenant. He, therefore, could not recover. The suit is dismissed with costs."

The haunted house remained untenanted for a long time. The proprietor subsequently made a gift of it to a charitable institution. The founders of this institution, who were Hindus and firm believers in charms and exorcisms, had some religious ceremony performed on the premises. Afterwards the house was pulled down and on its site now stands one of the grandest buildings in the station, that cost fully ten thousand pounds. Only this morning I received a visit from a gentleman who lives in the building, referred to above, but evidently he has not even heard of the ghosts of the Judge, his wife, and his Indian ayah.

It is now nearly fifty years; but the missing baby has not been heard of. If it is alive it has grown into a fully developed man. But does he know the fate of his parents and his nurse?

The Disembodied Hand

In connection with "The Major's Lease" it will not be out of place to relate an account that appeared in the papers some years ago.

A certain European gentleman was posted to a district in the Madras Presidency as a Government servant in the Financial Department.

When this gentleman reached the station to which he had been posted he put up at the Club, as they usually do, and began to look out for a house, when he was informed that there was a haunted house in the neighbourhood. Being rather sceptical he decided to take this house, ghost or no ghost. He was given to understand by the members of the Club that this house was a bit out of the way and was infested at night with thieves and robbers who came to divide their booty in that house; and to guard against its being occupied by a tenant it had been given a bad reputation. The proprietor being a wealthy old native of the old school did not care to investigate. So our friend, whom we shall, for the purposes of this story, call Mr. Hunter, took the house at a fair rent.

The house was in charge of a Chaukidar (caretaker, porter or watchman) when it was vacant. Mr. Hunter engaged the same man as a night watchman for this house. This Chaukidar informed Mr. Hunter that the ghost appeared only one day in the year, namely, the 21st of September, and added that if Mr. Hunter kept out of the house on that night there would be no trouble.

"I always keep away on the night of the 21st September," said the watchman.

"And what kind of ghost is it?" asked Mr. Hunter.

"It is a European lady dressed in white," said the man.

"What does she do?" asked Mr. Hunter.

"Oh! she comes out of the room and calls you and asks you to follow her," said the man.

"Has anybody ever followed her?"

"Nobody that I know of, Sir," said the man. "The man who was here before me saw her and died from fear."

"Most wonderful! But why do not people follow her in a body?" asked Mr. Hunter.

"It is very easy to say that, Sir, but when you see her you will not like to follow her yourself. I have been in this house for over 20 years, lots of times European soldiers have passed the night of the 21st September, intending to follow her but when she actually comes nobody has ever ventured."

"Most wonderful! I shall follow her this time," said Mr. Hunter.

"As you please Sir," said the man and retired.

It was one of the duties of Mr. Hunter to distribute the pensions of all retired Government servants.

In this connection Mr. Hunter used to come in contact with a number of very old men in the station who attended his office to receive their pensions from him.

By questioning them Mr. Hunter got so far that the house had at one time been occupied by a European officer.

This officer had a young wife who fell in love with a

certain Captain Leslie. One night when the husband was out on tour (and not expected to return within a week) his wife was entertaining Captain Leslie. The gentleman returned unexpectedly and found his wife in the arms of the Captain.

He lost his self-control and attacked the couple with a meat chopper—the first weapon that came handy.

Captain Leslie moved away and then cleared out leaving the unfortunate wife at the mercy of the infuriated husband. He aimed a blow at her head which she warded off with her hand. But so severe was the blow that the hand was cut off and the woman fell down on the ground quite unconscious. The sight of blood made the husband mad. Subsequently the servants came up and called a doctor, but by the time the doctor arrived the woman was dead.

The unfortunate husband who had become raving mad was sent to a lunatic asylum and thence taken away to England. The body of the woman was in the local cemetery; but what had become of the severed hand was not known. The missing limb had never been found. All this was 50 years ago, that is, immediately after the Indian Mutiny.

This was what Mr. Hunter gathered.

The 21st September was not very far off. Mr. Hunter decided to meet the ghost.

The night in question arrived, and Mr. Hunter sat in his bed-room with his magazine. The lamp was burning brightly.

The servants had all retired, and Mr. Hunter knew that if he called for help nobody would hear him, and even if anybody did hear, he too would not come.

He was, however, a very bold man and sat there awaiting developments.

At one in the morning he heard footsteps approaching the bed-room from the direction of the dining-room.

He could distinctly hear the rustle of the skirts. Gradually the door between the two rooms began to open wide. Then the curtain began to move. Mr. Hunter sat with straining eyes and beating heart.

At last she came in. The Englishwoman in flowing white robes. Mr. Hunter sat panting unable to move. She looked at him for about a minute and beckoned him to follow her. It was then that Mr. Hunter observed that she had only one hand.

He got up and followed her. She went back to the dining-room and he followed her there. There was no light in the dining-room but he could see her faintly in the dark. She went right across the dining-room to the door on the other side which opened on the verandah. Mr. Hunter could not see what she was doing at the door, but he knew she was opening it.

When the door opened she passed out and Mr. Hunter followed. Then she walked across the verandah down the steps and stood upon the lawn. Mr. Hunter was on the lawn in a moment. His fears had now completely vanished. She next proceeded along the lawn in the direction of a hedge. Mr. Hunter also reached the hedge and found that under the hedge were concealed two spades. The gardener must have been working with them and left them there after the day's work.

The lady made a sign to him and he took up one of the spades. Then again she proceeded and he followed.

They had reached some distance in the garden when the lady with her foot indicated a spot and Mr. Hunter inferred that she wanted him to dig there. Of course, Mr. Hunter knew that he was not going to discover a treasure-trove, but he was sure he was going to find something very interesting. So he began digging with all his vigour. Only about 18 inches below the surface the blade struck against some hard substance. Mr. Hunter looked up.

The apparition had vanished. Mr. Hunter dug on and discovered that the hard substance was a human hand with the fingers and everything intact. Of course, the flesh had gone, only the bones remained. Mr. Hunter picked up the bones and knew exactly what to do.

He returned to the house, dressed himself up in his cycling costume and rode away with the bones and the spade to the cemetery. He waked the night watchman, got the gate opened, found out the tomb of the murdered woman and close to it interred the bones, that he had found in such a mysterious fashion, reciting as much of the service as he could remember. Then he paid some buksheesh (reward) to the night watchman and came home.

He put back the spade in its old place and retired. A few days after he paid a visit to the cemetery in the day-time and found that grass had grown on the spot which he had dug up. The bones had evidently not been disturbed.

The next year on the 21st September Mr. Hunter kept up the whole night, but he had no visit from the ghostly lady.

The house is now in the occupation of another European gentleman who took it after Mr. Hunter's transfer from the station and this new tenant had no visit from the ghost either. Let us hope that *she* now rests in peace.

The Leaping Woman

The following extract from a Bengal newspaper that appeared in September 1913, is very interesting and instructive.

"The following extraordinary phenomenon took place at the Hooghly Police Club Building, Chinsurah, at about midnight on last Saturday.

"At this late hour of the night some peculiar sounds of agony on the roof of the house aroused the resident members of the Club, who at once proceeded to the roof with lamps and found to their entire surprise a lady clad in white jumping from the roof to the ground (about a hundred feet in height) followed by a man with a dagger in his hands. But eventually no trace of it could be found on the ground. This is not the first occasion that such beings are found to visit this house and it is heard from a reliable source that long ago a woman committed suicide by hanging and it is believed that her spirit loiters round the building. As these incidents have made a deep impression upon the members, they have decided to remove the Club from the said buildings."

The Open Door

Here again is something that is very peculiar and not very uncommon.

We, myself and three other friends of mine, were asked by another friend of ours to pass a week's holiday at the suburban residence of the last named. We took an evening train after the office hours and reached our destination at about 10-30 at night. The place was about 60 miles from Calcutta.

Our host had a very large house with a number of disused wings. I do not think many of my readers have any idea of a large residential house in Bengal. Generally it is a quadrangular sort of thing with a big yard in the centre which is called the "Angan" or "uthan" (a court-yard). On all sides of the court-yard are rooms of all sorts of shapes and sizes. There are generally two stories—the lower used as kitchen, godown, store-room, etc., and the upper as bed-rooms, etc.

Now this particular house of our friend was of the kind described above. It stood on extensive grounds wooded with fruit and timber trees. There was also a big tank, a miniature lake in fact, which was the property of my friend. There was good fishing in the lake and that was the particular attraction that had drawn my other friends to this place. I myself was not very fond of angling.

As I have said we reached this place at about 10-30 at night. We were received very kindly by the father and the mother of our host who were a very jolly old couple; and after a very late supper, or, shall I call it dinner, we retired. The guest rooms were well furnished and very comfortable. It was a bright moonlight night and our plan was to get up at 4 in the morning and go to the lake for angling.

At three in the morning the servants of our host woke us up (they had come to carry our fishing gear) and we went to the lake which was a couple of hundred yards from the house. As I have said it was a bright moonlight night in summer and the outing was not unpleasant after all. We remained on the bank of the lake till about seven in the morning, when one of the servants came to fetch us for our morning tea. I may as well mention here that breakfast in India generally means a pretty heavy meal at about 10 A.M.

I was the first to get up; for I have said already that I was not a worthy disciple of Izaak Walton. I wound up my line and walked away, carrying my rod myself.

The lake was towards the back of the house. To come from the lake to the front of it we had to pass along the whole length of the buildings. See the rough plan on the next page.

As would appear from the plan we had to pass along the shady foot-path ABCDE, there was a turning at each point B, C, D and E. The back row of rooms was used for go-downs, store-rooms, kitchens, etc. One room, the one with a door marked "★" at the corner, was used for storing a number of door-frames. The owner of the house, our host's father, had at one time contemplated adding a new wing and for that purpose the door-frames had been made. Then

The Open Door

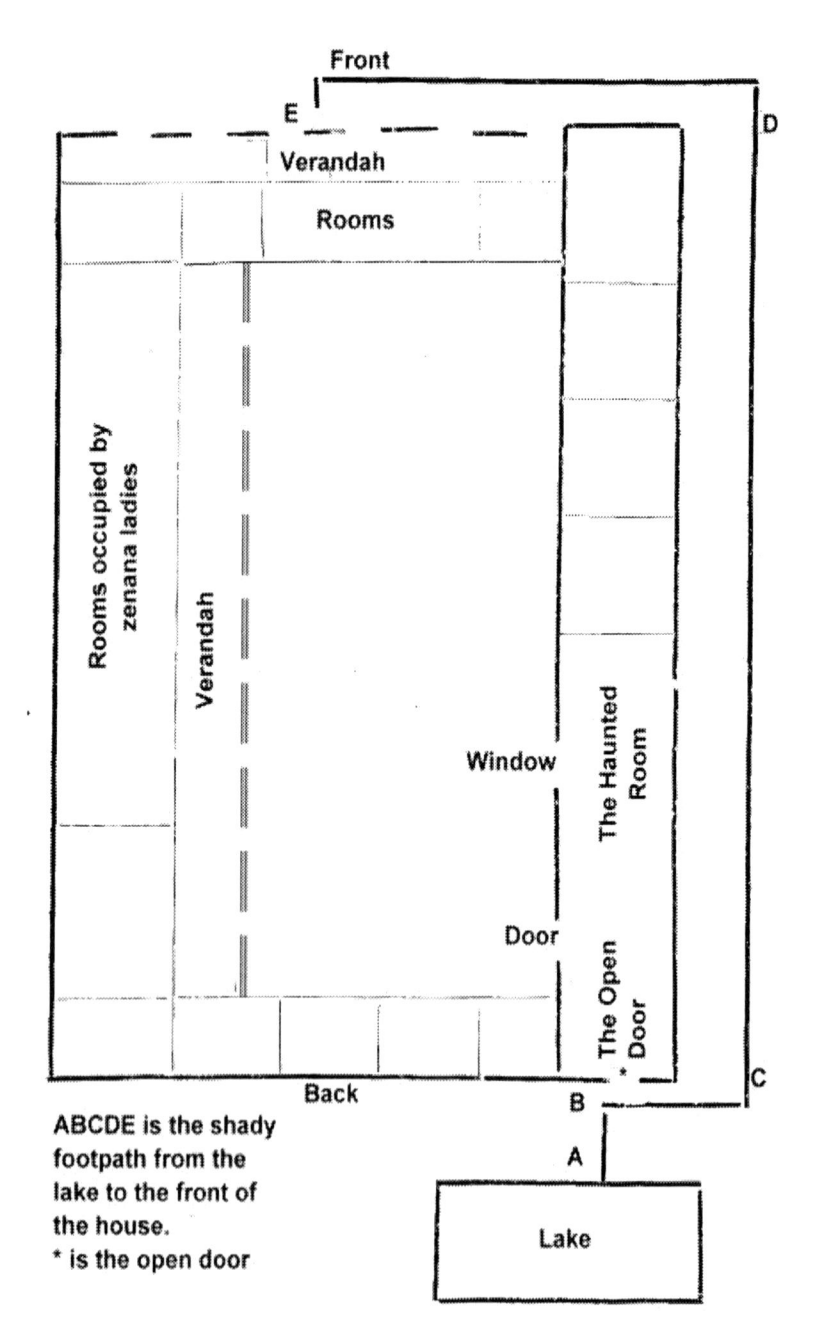

Front

E

Verandah

Rooms

Rooms occupied by zenana ladies

Verandah

Window

The Haunted Room

Door

The Open Door

Back

B

A

D

C

Lake

ABCDE is the shady footpath from the lake to the front of the house.
* is the open door

he gave up the idea and the door-frames were kept stored up in that corner-room with a door on the outside marked "★". Now as I was walking ahead I reached the turning B first of all and it was probably an accident that the point of my rod touched the door. The door flew open. I knew this was an unused portion of the house and so the opening of the door surprised me to a certain extent. I looked into the room and discovered the wooden door-frames. There was nothing peculiar about the room or its contents either.

When we were drinking our tea five minutes later I casually remarked that they would find some of the door-frames missing as the door of the room in which they were kept had been left open all night. I did not at that time attach any importance to a peculiar look of the eyes of the old couple, my host's father and mother. The old gentleman called one of the servants and ordered him to bolt that door.

When we were going to the lake in the evening I examined the door and found that it had been closed from inside.

The next morning we went out a-fishing again and we were returning for our tea, at about 7 in the morning. I was again ahead of all the rest. As I came along, this time intentionally I gave a push to the door with my rod. It again flew open. "This is funny" I thought.

At tea I reported the matter to the old couple and I then noticed with curiosity their embarrassed look of the day before. I therefore suggested that the servants intentionally left the door open, and one morning they would find the door-frames, stored in the room, gone.

At this the old man smiled. He said that the door of this particular room had remained open for the last 15 years and the contents had never been disturbed. On our pressing him why the door remained open he admitted with great reluctance that since the death of a certain servant of the house-hold in that particular room fifteen years ago the outer door had never remained closed.

"You may close it yourself and see" suggested the old gentleman.

We required no further invitation. Immediately we all went to that room to investigate and find out the ghost if he remained indoors during the day. But Mr. Ghost was not there.

"He has gone out for his morning constitutional," I suggested, "and this time we shall keep him out."

Now this particular room had two doors and one window. The window and one door were on the court-yard side of the room and communicated with the court-yard. The other door led to the grounds outside and this last was the haunted door. We opened both the doors and the window and examined the room. There was nothing extraordinary about it. Then we tried to close the haunted door. It had warped probably by being kept open for 15 years. It had two very strong bolts on the inside but the lower bolt would not go within 3 inches of its socket. The upper one was very loose and a little continuous thumping would bring the bolt down. We thought we had solved the mystery thus:—The servants only closed the door by pushing up the upper bolt, at night the wind would shake the door and the bolt would come down. So this time we took good care to use the lower bolt. Three of us pushed the door with all our might and one man thrust the lower bolt into its socket. It hardly went in a quarter of an inch, but still the door was secure. We then hammered the bolt in with bricks. In doing this we broke about half a dozen of them. This will explain to the reader how much strength it required to drive the bolt in about an inch and a half.

Then we satisfied ourselves that the bolt could not be moved without the aid of a hammer and a lever. Afterwards we closed the window and the other door and securely locked the last. Thus no human being could open the haunted door.

Before retiring to bed after dinner we further examined both the doors once more. They were all right.

The next morning we did not go out for fishing; so when we got up at about five in the morning the first thing we did was to go and examine the haunted door. It flew in at the touch. We then went inside and examined the other door and the window which communicated with the court-yard. The window was as secure as we had left it and the door was chained from outside. We went round into the court-yard and examined the lock. It did not appear to have been tampered with.

The old man and his wife met us at tea as usual. They had evidently been told everything. They, however, did not mention the subject, neither did we.

It was my intention to pass a night in that room but nobody would agree to bear me company, and I did not quite like the idea of passing a whole night in that ugly room. Moreover my hosts would not have heard of it.

The mystery of the open door has not yet been solved. It was about 20 years ago that what I have narrated above, happened. I am not sure that the mystery will ever be solved.

The Sleeper

Here's another tale about another family and another house in another part of Bengal.

Once while coming back from Darjeeling, the summer capital of Bengal, I had a very garrulous old gentleman for a fellow traveller in the same compartment. I was reading a copy of the Occult Review and the title of the magazine interested him very much. He asked me what the magazine was about, and I told him. He then asked me if I was really interested in ghosts and their stories. I told him that I was.

"In our village we have a gentleman who has a family ghost" said my companion.

"What kind of thing is a family ghost?" I asked.

"Oh—the ghost comes and has his dinner with my neighbour every night," said my companion. "Really—must be a very funny ghost" I said. "It is a fact—if you stay for a day in my village you will learn everything."

I at once decided to break my journey in the village. It was about 2 in the afternoon when I got down at the Railway Station—procured a hackney carriage and, ascertaining the name and address of the gentleman who had the family ghost, separated from my old companion.

I reached the house in 20 minutes, and told the gentleman that I was a stranger in those parts and as such craved leave to pass the rest of the day and the night under his roof.

I was a very unwelcome guest, but he could not kick me out, as the moral code would not permit it. He, however, shrewdly guessed why I was anxious to pass the night at his house.

Of course, my host was very kind to me. He was a tolerably rich man with a large family. Most of his sons were grown-up young men who were at College in Calcutta. The younger children were of course at home.

At night when we sat down to dinner I gently broached the subject by hinting at the rumour I had heard that his house was haunted. I further explained to him that I had only come to ascertain if what I had heard was true. He told me (of course it was very kind of him) that the story about the dinner was false, and what really happened was this:—

"I had a younger brother who died 2 years ago. He was of a religious turn of mind and passed his time in reading religious books and writing articles about religion in papers. He died suddenly one night. In fact he was found dead in his bed in the morning. The doctors said it was due to failure of heart. Since his death he has come and slept in the room, which was his when he was alive and is his still. All that he takes is a glass of water fetched from the sacred river Ganges. We put the glass of water in the room and make the bed every evening; the next morning the glass is found empty and the bed appears to have been slept upon."

"But why did you begin?—" I asked.

"Oh—One night he appeared to me in a dream and asked me to keep the water and a clean bed in the room—this was about a month after his death," said my host.

"Has anybody ever passed a night in the room to see what really happens?" I asked.

"His young wife—or rather widow passed a night in that room—the next morning we found her on the bed—sleeping—dead—from failure of heart—so the doctors said."

"Most wonderful and interesting." I remarked.

"Nobody has gone to that part of the house since the death of the poor young widow" said my host. "I have got all the doors of the room securely screwed up except one, and that too is kept carefully locked, and the key is always with me."

After dinner my host took me to the haunted room. All arrangements for the night were being made; and the bed was neat and clean.

A glass of the Ganges water was kept in a corner with a cover on it. I looked at the doors, they were all perfectly secure. The only door that could open was then closed and locked.

My host smiled at me sadly "we won't do all this uselessly" he said "this is a very costly trick if you think it a trick at all, because I have to pay to the servants double the amount that others pay in this village—otherwise they would run away. You can sleep at the door and see that nobody gets in at night."

I said "I believe you most implicitly and need not take the precaution suggested." I was then shown into my room and everybody withdrew.

My room was 4 or 5 apartments off and of course these apartments were to be unoccupied.

As soon as my host and the servants had withdrawn, I took up my candle and went to the locked door of the ghostly room. With the lighted candle I covered the back of the lock with a thin coating of soot or lamp-black. Then I scraped off a little dried-up whitewash from the wall and sprinkled the powder over the lamp-black.

"If any body disturbs the lock at night I shall know it in the morning" I thought. Well, the reader could guess that I had not a good sleep that night. I got up at about 4-30 in the morning and went to the locked door. My seal was intact, that is, the lamp-black with the powdered lime was there just as I had left it.

I took out my handkerchief and wiped the lock clean. The whole operation took me about 5 minutes. Then I waited.

At about 5 my host came and a servant with him. The locked door was opened in my presence. The glass of water was dry and there was not a drop of water in it. The bed had been slept upon. There was a distinct mark on the pillow where the head should have been—and the sheet too looked as if somebody had been in bed the whole night.

I left the same day by the after-noon train having passed about 23 hours with the family in the haunted house.

What Uncle Saw

> This story need not have been written. It is too sad and too mysterious, but since reference has been made to it in this book, it is only right that readers should know this sad account.

Uncle was a very strong and powerful man and used to boast a good deal of his strength. He was employed in a Government Office in Calcutta. He used to come to his village home during the holidays. He was a widower with one or two children, who stayed with his brother's family in the village.

Uncle has had no bed-room of his own since his wife's death. Whenever he paid us a visit one of us used to place his bed-room at uncle's disposal. It is a custom in Bengal to sleep with one's wife and children in the same bed-room. So whenever Uncle turned up I used to give my bed-room to him as I was the only person without children. On such occasions I slept in one of the "Baithaks" (drawing-rooms). A Baithak is a drawing-room and guest-room combined.

In rich Bengal families of the orthodox style the "Baithak" or "Baithak khana" is a very large room generally devoid of all furniture, having a thick rich carpet on the floor with a clean sheet upon it and big takias (pillows) all around the wall. The elderly people would sit on the ground and lean against the takias; while we, the younger lot, sat upon the takias and leaned against the wall which in the case of the particular room in our house was covered with some kind of yellow paint which did not come off on the clothes.

Sometimes a takia would burst and the cotton stuffing inside would come out; and then the old servant (his status is that of an English butler, his duty to prepare the hookah for the master) would give us a chase with a lathi (stick) and the offender would run away, and not return until all incriminating evidence had been removed and the old servant's wrath had subsided.

Well, when Uncle used to come I slept in the "Baithak" and my wife slept somewhere in the zenana, I never inquired where.

On this particular occasion Uncle missed the train by which he usually came. It was the month of October and he should have arrived at 8 P.M. My bed had been made in the Baithak. But the 8 P.M. train came and stopped and passed on and Uncle did not turn up.

So we thought he had been detained for the night. It was the Durgapooja season and some presents for the children at home had to be purchased and, we thought, that was what was detaining him. And so at about 10 P.M. we all retired to bed. The bed that had been made for me in the "Baithak" remained there for Uncle in case he turned up by the 11 P.M. train. As a matter of fact we did not expect him till the next morning.

But as misfortune would have it Uncle did arrive by the 11 o'clock train.

All the house-hold had retired, and though the old servant suggested that I should be waked up, Uncle would not hear of it. He would sleep in the bed originally made for me, he said.

The bed was in the central Baithak or hall. My Uncle was very fond of sleeping in side-rooms. I do not know why. Anyhow he ordered the servant to remove his bed to one of the side-rooms. Accordingly the bed was taken to one of them. One side of that room had two windows opening on the garden. The garden was more a park-like place, rather neglected, but still well wooded abounding in jack fruit trees. It used to be quite shady and dark during the day there. On this particular night it must have been very dark. I do not remember now whether there was a moon or not.

Well, Uncle went to sleep and so did the servants. It was about 8 o'clock the next morning, when we thought that Uncle had slept long enough, that we went to wake him up.

The door connecting the side-room with the main Baithak was closed, but not bolted from inside; so we pushed the door open and went in.

Uncle lay in bed panting. He stared at us with eyes that saw but did not perceive. We at once knew that something was wrong. On touching his body we found that he had high fever. We opened the windows, and it was then that Uncle spoke "Don't open or it would come in—"

"What would come in Uncle—what?" we asked.

But uncle had fainted.

The doctor was called in. He arrived at about ten in the morning. He said it was high fever—due to what he could not say. All the same he prescribed a medicine.

The medicine had the effect of reducing the temperature, and at about 6 in the evening consciousness returned. Still he was in a very weak condition. Some medicine was given to induce sleep and he passed the night well. We nursed him by turns at night. The next morning we had all the satisfaction of seeing him all right. He walked from the bed-room, though still very weak and came to the Central Baithak where he had tea with us. It was then that we asked what he had seen and what he had meant by "It would come in."

Oh how we wish, we had never asked him the question, at least then.

This was what he said:—

"After I had gone to bed I found that there were a few mosquitoes and so I could not sleep well. It was about midnight when they gradually disappeared and then I began to fall asleep. But just as I was dozing off I heard somebody strike the bars of the windows thrice. It was like three distinct strokes with a cane on the gratings outside. 'Who is there?' I asked; but no reply. The striking stopped. Again I closed my eyes and again the same strokes were repeated. This time I nearly lost my temper; I thought it was some urchin of the neighbourhood in a mischievous mood. 'Who is there?' I again shouted—again no reply. The striking however stopped. But after a time it commenced afresh. This time I lost my temper completely and opened the window, determined to thrash anybody whom I found there—forgetting that the windows were barred and fully 6 feet above the ground. Well in the darkness I saw, I saw—."

Here uncle had a fit of shivering and panting, and within a minute he lost all consciousness. The fever was again high. The doctor was summoned but this time his medicines did no good. Uncle never regained consciousness. In fact after 24 hours he died of heart failure the next morning, leaving his story unfinished and without in any way giving us an idea of what that terrible thing was which he had seen beyond the window. The whole thing remains a deep mystery and unfortunately the mystery will never be solved.

Nobody has ventured to pass a night in the side-room since then. If I had not been a married man with a very young wife I might have tried.

One thing however remains and it is this that though uncle got all the fright in the world in that room, he neither came out of that room nor called for help.

One cry for help and the whole house-hold would have been awake. In fact there was a servant within 30 yards of the window which uncle had opened; and this man says he heard uncle open the window and close and bolt it again, though he had not heard uncle's shouts of "Who is there?"

The Weekend Wife

Only this morning I read this funny advertisement in the *Morning Post*.

> ## Haunted Houses
> Man and wife, cultured and travelled, gentle people—having lost fortune ready to act as caretakers and to investigate in view of removing trouble—.

Well—in a haunted house these gentle people expect to see something. Let us hope they will not see what our Uncle saw or what the Major saw.

This advertisement clearly shows that even in countries like England haunted houses do exist, or at least houses exist which are believed to be haunted.

If what we see really depends on what we think or what we believe, no wonder that there are so many more haunted houses in India than in England. This reminds me of a very old incident of my early school days. A boy was really caught by a Ghost and then there was trouble. We shall not forget the thrashing we received from our teacher in the school; and the fellow who was actually caught by the

Ghost—if Ghost it was, will never say in future that Ghosts don't exist.

In this connection it may not be out of place to narrate another incident, though it does not fall within the same category with the main story that heads this chapter. The only reason why I do so is that the facts tally in one respect, though in one respect only, and that is that the person who knew would tell nothing.

This was a friend of mine who was a widower. We were in the same office together and he occupied a chair and a table next but one to mine. This gentleman was in our office for only six months after narrating the story. If he had stayed longer we might have got out his secret, but unfortunately he went away; he has gone so far from us that probably we shall not meet again for the next 10 years.

It was in connection with the "Smith's dead wife's photograph" controversy that one day one of my fellow clerks told me that a visit from a dead wife was nothing very wonderful, as our friend Haralal could testify.

I always took of a lot of interest in ghosts and their stories. So I was generally at Haralal's desk cross-examining him about this affair; at first the gentleman was very uncommunicative but when he saw I would give him no rest he made a statement which I have every reason to believe is true. This is more or less what he says.

"It was about ten years ago that I joined this office. I have been a widower ever since I left college—in fact I married the daughter of a neighbour when I was at college and she died about 3 years afterwards, when I was just thinking of beginning life in right earnest. She has been dead these 10 years and I shall never marry again, (a young widower in good circumstances, in Bengal, is as rare as a blue rose).

"I have a suite of bachelor rooms in Calcutta, but I go to my suburban home on every Saturday afternoon and stay there till Monday morning, that is, I pass my Saturday night and the whole of Sunday in my village home every week.

"On this particular occasion nearly eight years ago, that is, about a year and a half after the death of my young wife I went home by an evening train. There is any number of trains in the evening and there is no certainty by which train I go, so if I am late, generally everybody goes to bed with the exception of my mother.

"On this particular night I reached home rather late. It was the month of September and there had been a heavy shower in the town and all tram-car services had been suspended.

"When I reached the Railway Station I found that the trains were not running to time either. I was given to understand that a tree had been blown down against the telegraph wire, and so the signals were not going through; and as it was rather dark the trains were only running on the report of a motor trolly that the line was clear. Thus I reached home at about eleven instead of eight in the evening.

"I found my father also sitting up for me though he had had his dinner. He wanted to learn the particulars of the storm at Calcutta.

"Within ten minutes of my arrival he went to bed and within an hour I finished my dinner and retired for the night.

"It was rather stuffy and the bed was damp as I was perspiring freely; and consequently I was not feeling inclined to sleep.

"A little after midnight I felt that there was somebody else in the room.

"I looked at the closed door—yes there was no mistake about it, it was my wife, my wife who had been dead these eighteen months.

"At first I was—well you can guess my feeling—then she spoke:

"'There is a cool bed-mat under the bedstead; it is rather dusty, but it will make you comfortable.

"I got up and looked under the bedstead—yes the cool bed-mat was there right enough and it was dusty too. I took it outside and I cleaned it by giving it a few jerks. Yes, I had to pass through the door at which she was standing within six inches of her,—don't put any questions; Let me tell you as much as I like; you will get nothing out of me if you interrupt—yes, I passed a comfortable night. She was in that room for a long time, telling me lots of things. The next morning my mother enquired with whom I was talking and I told her a lie. I said I was reading my novel aloud. They all know it at home now. She comes and passes two nights with me in the week when I am at home. She does not come to Calcutta. She talks about various matters and she is happy—don't ask me how I know that. I shall not tell you whether I have touched her body because that will give rise to further questions.

"Everybody at home has seen her, and they all know what I have told you, but nobody has spoken to her. They all respect and love her—nobody is afraid. In fact she never comes except on Saturday and Sunday evenings and that when I am at home."

No amount of cross-examination, coaxing or inducement made my friend Haralal say anything further.

This story in itself would not probably have been believed; but after the incident of "His dead wife's picture" nobody disbelieved it, and there is no reason why anybody should. Haralal is not a man who would tell yarns, and then I have made enquiries at Haralal's village where several persons know this much; that his dead wife pays him a visit twice every week.

Now that Haralal is 500 miles from his village home I do not know how things stand; but I am told that this story reached the ears of the Bara Saheb and he asked Haralal if he would object to a transfer and Haralal told him that he would not.

I shall leave the reader to draw his own conclusions.

The Boy Who Was Caught

Nothing is more common in India than seeing a ghost. Every one of us has seen ghost at some period of his existence; and if we have not actually seen one, some other person has, and has given us such a vivid description that we cannot but believe to be true what we hear.

This is, however, my own experience. I am told others have observed the phenomenon before.

When we were boys at school we used, among other things, to discuss ghosts. Most of my fellow students asserted that they did not believe in ghosts, but I was one of those who not only believed in their existence but also in their power to do harm to human beings if they liked. Of course, I was in the minority. As a matter of fact I knew that all those who said that they did not believe in ghosts told a lie. They believed in ghosts as much as I did, only they had not the courage to admit their weakness and differ boldly from the sceptics. Among the lot of unbelievers was one Ram Lal, a student of the Fifth Standard, who swore that he did not believe in ghosts and further that he would do anything to convince us that they did not exist.

It was, therefore, at my suggestion that he decided to go one moon-light night and hammer down a wooden peg into the soft sandy soil of the Hindoo Burning Ghat, it being well known that the ghosts generally put in a visible appearance at a burning ghat on a moon-light night. (A burning ghat is the place where dead bodies of Hindoos are cremated).

It was the warm month of April and the river had shrunk into the size of a nullah or drain. The real pukka ghat (the bathing place, built of bricks and lime) was about 200 yards from the water of the main stream, with a stretch of sand between.

The ghats are only used in the morning when people come to bathe, and in the evening they are all deserted. After a game of football on the school grounds we sometimes used to come and sit on the pukka ghat for an hour and return home after nightfall.

Now, it was the 23rd of April and a bright moon-light night, every one of us (there were about a dozen) had told the people at home that there was a function at the school and he might be late. On this night, it was arranged that the ghost test should take place.

The boy who had challenged the ghost, Ram Lal, was to join us at the pukka ghat at 8 P.M.; and then while we waited there he would walk across the sand and drive the peg into the ground at the place where a dead body had been cremated that very morning. We were to supply the peg and the hammer. (I had to pay the school gardener two annas for the loan of a peg and a hammer).

Well, we procured the peg and the hammer and proceeded to the pukka ghat. If the gardener had known what we required the peg and the hammer for, I am sure he would not have lent these to us.

Though I was a firm believer in ghosts yet I did not expect that Ram Lal would be caught. What I hoped for was that he would not turn up at the trysting place. But to my disappointment Ram Lal did turn up and at the appointed hour too. He came boasting as usual, took the peg and the hammer and started across the sand saying that he would break the head of any ghost who might venture within the reach of the hammerhead. Well, he went along and we waited for his return at the pukka ghat. It was a glorious night, the whole expanse of sand was shining in the bright moonlight.

On and on went Ram Lal with the peg in his left hand and the hammer in his right. He was dressed in the usual upcountry Indian style, in a long coat or Achkan which reached well below his knees and fluttered in the breeze.

As he went on his pace slackened. When he had gone about half the distance he stopped and looked back. We hoped he would return. He put down the hammer and the peg, sat down on the sand facing us, took off his shoes. Only some sand had got in. He took up the peg and hammer and walked on.

But then we felt that his courage was oozing away. Another fifty yards and he again stopped, and looked back at us.

Another fifty yards remained. Will he return? No! he again proceeded, but we could clearly see that his steps were less jaunty than when he had started. We knew that he was trembling, we knew that he would have blessed us to call him back. But we would not yield, neither would he. Looking in our direction at every step he proceeded and reached the burning ghat. He reached the identical spot where the pyre had been erected in the morning.

There was very little breeze,—not a mouse stirring. Not a soul was within 200 yards of him and he could not expect much help from us. How poor Ram Lal's heart must have palpitated! When we see Ram Lal now how we feel that we should burst.

Well, Ram Lal knelt down, fixed the peg in the wet sandy soil and began hammering. After each stroke he looked at us and at the river and in all directions. He struck blow after blow and we counted about thirty. That his hands had become nerveless we would understand, for otherwise a dozen strokes should have been enough to make the peg vanish in the soft sandy soil.

The peg went in and only about a couple of inches remained visible above the surface; and then Ram Lal thought of coming back. He was kneeling still. He tried to stand up, gave out a shrill cry for help and fell down face foremost.

It must have been his cry for help that made us forget our fear of the ghost, and we all ran at top speed towards the ghat. It was rather difficult to run fast on the sand but we managed it as well as we could, and stopped only when we were about half a dozen yards from the unconscious form of Ram Lal.

There he lay senseless as if gone to sleep. Our instinct told us that he was not dead. We thanked God, and each one of us sent up a silent prayer. Then we cried for help and a boatman who lived a quarter of a mile away came up. He took up Ram Lal in his arms and as he was doing it tr--rrrrrrrrrr—went Ram Lal's long coat. The unfortunate lad had hammered the skirt of his long coat along with the peg into the ground.

We took Ram Lal to his house and explained to his mother that he had a bad fall in the football field, and there we left him.

The next morning at school, one student, who was a neighbour of Ram Lal, told us that the whole mischief had become known.

Ram Lal, it appears, got high fever immediately after we

had left him and about midnight he became delirious and in that condition he disclosed everything in connection with his adventure at the ghat.

In the evening we went to see him. His parents were very angry with us.

The whole story reached the ears of the school authorities and we got, what I thought I richly deserved (for having allowed any mortal being to defy a ghost) but what I need not say.

Ram Lal is now a grown up young man. He holds a responsible government appointment and I meet him sometimes when he comes to tour in our part of the Province.

I always ask him if he has seen a ghost since we met last.

Two Ghosts

Here are two simple tales, one from my own experiences and the other related to me by a friend.

I shall tell my friend's story first, in his own words.

"I used to go for a bath in the Ganges early every morning. I used to start from home at 4 o'clock in the morning and walked down to the Ganges which was about 3 miles from my house. The bath took about an hour and then I used to come back in my carriage which went for me at about six in the morning.

"On this eventful morning when I awoke it was brilliant moonlight and so I thought it was dawn.

"I started from home without looking at the clock and when I was about a mile and a half from home and about the same distance from the river I realized that I was rather early. The policeman under the railway bridge told me that it was only 2 o'clock. I knew that I should have to cross the small maidan through which the road ran and I remembered that there was a rumour that a ghost had sometimes been seen in the maidan and on the road. This however did not make me nervous, because I really did not believe in ghosts; but all the same I wished I could have gone back. But then in going back I should have to pass the policeman and he would think that I was afraid; so I decided to go on.

"When I entered the maidan a creepy sensation came over me. My first idea was that I was being followed, but I did not dare look back, all the same I went on with quick steps.

"My next idea was that a gust of wind swept past me, and then I thought that a huge form was passing over the trees which lined the road.

"By this time I was in the middle of the maidan about half a mile from the nearest human being.

"And then, horror of horrors, the huge form came down from the trees and stood in the middle of the road about a hundred yards ahead of me, barring my way.

"I instinctively moved to the side—but did not stop. By the time I reached the spot, I had left the metalled portion of the road and was actually passing under the road-side trees allowing their thick trunks to intervene between me and the huge form standing in the middle of the road. I did not look at it, but I was sure it was extending a gigantic arm towards me. It could not, however, catch me and I walked on with vigorous strides. After I had passed the figure I nearly ran under the trees, my heart beating like a sledge hammer within me.

"After a couple of minutes I saw two glaring eyes in front of me. This I thought was the end. The eyes were advancing towards me at a rapid pace and then I heard a shout like that of a cow in distress. I stopped where I was. I hoped the ghost would pass along the road overlooking me. But when the ghost was within say fifty yards of me it gave another howl and I knew that it had seen me. A cry for help escaped my lips and I fainted.

"When I regained consciousness I found myself on the grassy foot-path by the side of the road, about 4 or 5 human beings hovering about me and a motor car standing near.

"Then the whole mystery became clear as day-light. The eyes that I had seen were the headlights of the 24 H.P. Silent Knight Minerva of Captain———. He had gone on a pleasure-trip to the next station and was returning home with two friends and his wife in his motor car when in that part of the road he saw something like a man standing in the middle of the road and sounded his horn. As the figure in the middle of the road would not move aside he slowed down and then heard my cry.

"The rest the reader may guess. The figure that had loomed so large with out-stretched arm was only a municipal danger signal erected in the middle of the road. A red lamp had been placed on the top of the erection but it had been blown out."

This was the whole story of my friend. It shows how even our prosaic but overwrought imagination sometimes gives to airy nothings a local habitation and a name. My own personal experience which I shall describe now will also, I am sure, be interesting.

It was on a brilliant moon-light night in the month of June that we were sleeping in the open court-yard of our house.

Of course, the courtyard had a wall all round with a partition in the middle; on one side of the partition slept three girls of the family and on the other were the younger male members, four in number.

It was our custom to have a long chat after dinner and before retiring to bed.

On this particular night the talk had been about ghosts. Of course, the girls are always ready to believe everything and so when we left them we knew that they would not sleep very comfortably that night. We retired to our part of the court-yard, but we could overhear the conversation of the girls. One was trying to convince the other two that ghosts did not exist and if they did exist they never came into contact with human beings.

Then we fell asleep.

How long we had slept we did not know, but a sudden cry from, one of the girls awoke us and within three seconds we were across the low partition wall, and with her. She was sitting up in bed pointing with her fingers. Following the direction we saw in the clear moonlight the figure of a short woman standing in the corner of the court-yard about 20 yards from us pointing her finger at something (not towards us).

We looked in that direction bub could see nothing peculiar there.

Our first idea was that it was one of the maid-servants,

who had heard our after-dinner conversation, playing the ghost. But this particular ghostly lady was very short, much shorter than any servant in the establishment. After some, hesitation all (four) of us advanced towards the ghost. I remember how my heart throbbed as I advanced with the other three boys.

Then we laughed loud and long.

What do you think it was?

It was only the Lawn Tennis net wrapped round the pole standing against the wall. The handle of the ratchet arrangement looked like an extending finger.

But from a distance in the moon-light it looked exactly like a short woman draped in white.

This story again shows what trick our imagination plays with us at times.

The Haunted Well

Here's a very funny story told by a friend of my grandfather—a famous medical man of Calcutta.

This famous doctor was once sent for to treat a gentleman at Agra. This gentleman was a rich Marwari who was suffering from indigestion. When the doctor reached Agra he was lodged in very comfortable quarters and a number of horses and carriages was placed at his disposal.

He was informed that the patient had been treated by all the local and provincial practitioners but without any result.

The doctor who was as clever a man of the world as of medicine, at once saw that there was really nothing the matter with the patient. He was really suffering from a curious malady which could in a phrase be called—"want of physical exercise."

Agra, the city after which the Province is named, abounds in old magnificent buildings which it takes the tourist a considerable time to see, and the Doctor, of course, was enjoying all the sights in the meantime.

He also prescribed a number of medicines which proved of no avail. The Doctor had anticipated it, and so he had decided what medicine he would prescribe next.

During the sight-seeing excursions into the environs of the city the doctor had discovered a large pukka well not

The Haunted Well

far from a main street and at a distance of 3 miles from his patient's house.

This was a very old disused well and it was generally rumoured that a ghost dwelt in it. So nobody would go near the well at night. Of course, there was a lot of stories as to what the ghost looked like and how he came out at times and stood on the brink and all that,—but the doctor really did not believe any of these. He, however, believed that this ghost, (whether there really was any or not in that well) would cure his patient.

So one morning when he saw his patient he said "Lalla Saheb—I have found out the real cause of your trouble—it is a ghost whom you have got to propitiate and unless you do that you will never get well—and no medicine will help you and your digestion will never improve."

"A Ghost?" asked the patient.

"A Ghost!" exclaimed the people around.

"A Ghost" said the doctor sagely.

"What shall I have to do?" inquired the patient, anxiously—

"You will have to go every morning to that well (indicating the one mentioned above), and throw a basketful of flowers in" said the doctor.

"I shall do that every day" said the patient.

"Then we shall begin from tomorrow" said the doctor.

The next morning everybody had been ready to start long before the doctor was out of bed. He came at last and all got up to start. Then a big landau and pair drew up to take the doctor and the patient to the abode of the ghost in the well. Just as the patient was thinking of getting in the doctor said "We don't require a carriage Lalla Saheb—we shall all have to walk—and bare-footed too, and between you and me we shall have to carry the basket of flowers also."

The patient was really troubled. Never indeed in his life had he walked a mile—not to say of three—and that, bare-footed and carrying a basket of flowers in his hands. However he had to do it. It was a goodly procession. The big millionaire—the big doctor with a large number of followers walking bare-footed—caused amazement and amusement to all who saw them.

It took them a full hour and a half to reach the well—and there the doctor pronounced the mantra in Sanskrit and the flowers were thrown in. The mantra (charm) was in Sanskrit, the doctor who knew a little of the language had taken great pains to compose it the night before and even then it was not grammatically quite correct.

At last the party returned, but not on foot. The journey back was performed in the carriages that had followed the patient and his doctor. From that day the practice was followed regularly. The patient's health began to improve and he began to regain his power of digestion fast. In a month he was all right; but he never discontinued the practice of going to the well and throwing in a basketful of flowers with his own hands. He had also learnt the mantra (the mystic charm) by heart; but the doctor had sworn him to secrecy and he told it to nobody. Shoes with felt sole were soon procured from England (it being 40 years before any Indian Rope Sole Shoe Factory came into existence) and thus the inconvenience of walking this distance bare-footed was easily obviated.

After a month's further stay the doctor came away from Agra having earned a fabulous fee, and he always received occasional letters and presents from his patient who never discontinued the practice of visiting the well till his death about 17 years later.

"The three-mile walk is all that he requires" said the doctor to his friends (among whom evidently my grandfather was one) on his return from Agra, "and since he has got used to it now he won't discontinue even if he comes to know of the deception I have practised on him—and I have cured his indigestion after all."

The patient, of course, never discovered the fraud. He never gave the matter his serious consideration. His friends, who were as ignorant and prejudiced as he himself was, believed in the ghost as much as he did himself. The medical practitioners of Agra who probably were in the Doctor's secret never told him anything—and if they had told him anything they would probably have heard language from Our patient that could not well be described as quite parliamentary, for they had all tried to cure him and failed.

The Strange Tree

This tale will show how much "imagination" works upon the external organs of a human being.

If a person goes about with the idea that there is a ghost somewhere about he will probably see the ghost in everything.

But has it ever struck the reader that sometimes horses and dogs do not quite enjoy going to a place which is reputed to be haunted?

In a village in Bengal not far from my home there is a big Jack-fruit tree which is said to be haunted.

I visited this place once—the local zamindar had sent me his elephant. The Gomashta (estate manager) who knew that I had come to see the haunted tree, told me that I should probably see nothing during the day, but the elephant would not go near the tree.

I passed the tree. It was about 3 miles from the Railway Station. There was nothing extraordinary about it. This was about 11 o'clock in the morning. Then I went to the Shooting Box (usually called the Cutchery or Court house—where the zamindars and their servants put up when they pay a visit to this part of their possessions) to have my bath and breakfast most hospitably provided by my generous host. I ordered the elephant to be put under this tree, and this was done though the people there told me that the elephant would not remain there long.

At about 2 P.M. I heard an extraordinary noise from the tree.

It was only the elephant. It was wailing and was looking as bad as it possibly could.

We all went there but found nothing. The elephant was not ill.

I ordered it to be taken away from under the tree. As soon as the chain was removed from the animal's foot it rushed away like a race horse and would not stop within 200 yards of the tree. I was vastly amused. I had never seen an elephant running before. But under the tree we found nothing. What made the elephant so afraid has remained a secret.

The servants told me (what I had heard before) that it was only elephants, horses and dogs that did not stay long under that tree. No human eyes have ever seen anything supernatural or fearful there.

The Starving Millionaire

This story was in the papers; it created a sensation at the time, now it has been almost forgotten. The story shows that black art with all its mysteries is not a thing of the past. This was what happened.

There was a certain rich European Contractor in the Central Provinces in India.

Let us call him Anderson. He used to supply stone ballast to the Railway Companies and had been doing this business for over a quarter of a century. He had accumulated wealth and was a multi-millionaire and one of the richest men in his part of the country. The district which he made his head quarters was a large one. It was a second class military station and there were two European regiments and one Indian regiment in that station. Necessarily there was a number of European military officers besides a number of civil and executive officers in that station.

On a certain June morning, which is a very hot month in India, an Indian Fakir came into the compound of Mr. Anderson begging for alms. Mr. Anderson and his wife were sitting in the verandah drinking their morning tea. It had been a very hot night and there being no electricity in this particular station, Mr. Anderson had to depend on the sleepy punkha coolie. The punkha coolie on this particular night was more sleepy than usual, and so Mr. Anderson had passed a very sleepless night indeed. He was in a very bad temper. A whole life passed among Indian workmen does not generally make a man good-tempered and a hot June in the Indian plains is not particularly conducive to sweet temper either. When this beggar came in Mr. Anderson was in a very bad mood. As the man walked fearlessly up to the verandah Mr. Anderson's temper became worse. He asked the beggar what he wanted. The beggar answered he wanted food. Of course, Mr. Anderson said he had nothing to give. The beggar replied that he would accept some money and buy the food. Mr. Anderson was not in the habit of being contradicted. He lost his temper—abused the beggar and ordered his servants to turn the man out. The servants obeyed. Before his departure the beggar turned to Mr. Anderson and told him that very soon he would know how painful it was to be hungry.

When the beggar was gone Mr. Anderson thought of his last remark and laughed. He was a well-known rich man and a good paymaster. An order for a £100 on a dirty slip of paper would be honoured by his banker without hesitation. Naturally he laughed. He forgot that men had committed suicide by drowning to avoid death from thirst. Well, there it was.

The bell announcing breakfast rang punctually at 10 o'clock in the morning. Mr. Anderson joined his wife in the drawing-room and they went to the dining-room together. The smell of eggs and bacon and coffee greeted them and Mr. Anderson forgot all about the Indian beggar when he took his seat. But he received a rude shock. There was a big live caterpillar in the fish. Mr. Anderson called the servant and ordered him to take away the fish and serve with eyes open the next time. The servant who had been in Mr.

Anderson's service a long time stared open-mouthed. Only a minute before there was nothing but fish on the plate. Whence came this ugly creature? Well, the plate was removed and another put in its place for the next dish. When the next dish came another surprise awaited everybody.

As the cover was removed it was found that the whole contents were covered with a thin layer of sweepings. The Khansama (the servant who serves at the table) looked at Mr. Anderson and Mr. Anderson at the Khansama "with a wild surmise"; the cover was replaced and the dish taken away. Nothing was said this time.

After about 5 minutes of waiting a third covered dish was brought.

When the cover was removed the contents were found mixed with stable sweepings. The smell was horrible, the dish was at once removed.

This was about the limit.

No man can eat after that. Mr. Anderson left the table and went to his office—without breakfast.

It was the habit of Mr. Anderson to have his lunch in his office. A Khansama used to take a tiffin basket to the office and there in his private room Mr. Anderson ate his lunch punctually at 2 P.M. Today he expected his tiffin early. He thought, that though he had left no instructions himself the Khansama would have the sense to remember that he had gone to office without breakfast. And so Mr. Anderson expected a lunch heavier than usual and earlier too.

But it was two o'clock and the servant had not arrived. Mr. Anderson was a man of particularly regular habits. He was very hungry. The thought of the beggar in the morning made him angry too. He shouted to his punkha coolie to pull harder.

It was a quarter after two and still the Khansama would not arrive. It was probably the first time in 20 years that the fellow was late. Mr. Anderson sent his chaprasi (peon) to look for the Khansama at about half past two. A couple of minutes after the chaprasi's departure, Mr. Atkins, the Collector of the district, was announced (A Collector is generally a District Magistrate also, and in the Central Provinces he is called the Deputy Commissioner). He is one of the principal officers in the district. In this particular district of which I am speaking there were two principal government officers. The Divisional Judge was the head of the Civil Administration as well as the person who tried the murderers and all other big offenders who deserved more than seven years imprisonment. He was a Bengal Brahman. Mr. Atkins was the Collector or rather the Deputy Commissioner. He was the executive head of the district. He was also the District Magistrate. Mr. Atkins came in and thus explained a sad accident which Mr. Anderson's Khansama had met with:

"As I was passing along the road in my motor car, your man came in the way and was knocked down. The man is hurt but not badly. He had been carrying a tiffin basket which was also knocked down, as a matter of course; and the car having passed over it everything the basket contained in the shape of china was smashed up. The man has been taken to the hospital by myself in an unconscious condition, but the doctor says there is nothing very serious, and he will be all right in a couple of days."

Now Mr. Atkins was a great friend of Mr. Anderson. They had known each other ever since Mr. Atkins's arrival in India as a young member of the Civil Service. That was over 20 years ago. He had at first been in that district for over 7 years as an Assistant Commissioner and this time he was there for over 3 years as a Deputy Commissioner. But Mr. Anderson was very hungry. The story of Mr. Atkins had given him the second shock since the morning. He, therefore, used language which no gentleman should have done; and with great vehemence threatened to prosecute Mr. Atkins for rash driving, etc.

Mr. Atkins was a very good-natured man. He knew the temper of Mr. Anderson; but he had never been Anderson so angry before. He therefore beat a hasty retreat, wondering whether Anderson had not gone mad. He would not have told anybody what happened in Anderson's offices if he had known the starving condition of the millionaire, but as it happened he repeated the fine language that Anderson had used, in the club that same evening. Everybody who heard his story opined at he time that Anderson was clearly off his head.

Mr. Anderson and his wife were expected at the club, but they did not turn up.

When Mr. Atkins went home he got a letter from Anderson in which the latter had apologised for what he had said in the office that afternoon. In the letter there was a sentence which was rather enigmatic:

"If you know what I am suffering from, Atkins, you will be sorry for me, not angry with me—I pray to God you may not suffer such—." The letter had evidently been written in great haste and had not been revised. Mr. Atkins did not quite understand the matter; and he intended to look up Anderson the first thing next morning. Mr. Atkins thought that Anderson had lost some of his money. He knew that Anderson never speculated. Still he might have suffered a heavy loss in one of his contracts. He telephoned to Mr. Anderson at his house, but was informed by one of the servants that the master had gone out in his motor car at six in the evening and was not back till then.

Now let us see what happened to Mr. Anderson after he had left his office at about four in the afternoon.

He went home and expected some tea, but no tea arrived, though it was six. The Khansama was in the hospital; the cook was called and he humbly offered the following explanation: "As soon as Hazoor (Your Honour) came back I ordered the khidmatgar (the cook's assistant) to put the kettle on the fire. (This is the ordinary duty of the khidmatgar). There was a bright coal fire in the stove, and the khidmatgar put the kettle upon it. The kettle should have boiled within five minutes, but it did not; your humble servant went to investigate the cause and found that there was no water in the kettle. We put in some, but the kettle had in the meantime become nearly red-hot. As soon as it came into contact with the cold water it burst like a bomb. Fortunately nobody was hurt.

There was, of course, a saucepan to heat some water in, but the cold water had got into the stove and extinguished it. It would be another half an hour before tea was ready, he added. Mr. Anderson now realised that it was not the fault of the servants but the curse of the Indian Fakir. So with a sad smile he ordered his motor car and thought that he and his wife had better try the Railway refreshment rooms. When his chauffeur was going to start the engine Mr. Anderson expected that there would be a backfire and the chauffeur would have a dislocated wrist. But there was no accident. The engine started as smoothly as it had never done before. Mr. and Mrs. Anderson went to the Railway refreshment rooms. There they were informed that no tea was available. A dead rat had been found under one of the tables in the first class refreshment room, and as plague cases had been reported earlier in the week, the station master had ordered the rooms to be closed till they had been thoroughly disinfected. The whole staff of waiters with all the preserved meat and oilman's stores had been sent by special train to the next station so that the railway passengers might not be inconvenienced. The next station was eight miles off and there was no road for a motor car.

"I had expected as much" said Mr. Anderson bitterly, as he left the Railway Station.

"I would go to Captain Fraser and beg for some dinner. He is the only man who has got a family here and will be able to accommodate us" said he to his wife, and so off they started for a five mile run to the Cantonments. There was some trouble with the car on the way and they were detained for about an hour, and it was actually 8-30 in the evening when the Andersons reached Captain Fraser's place. Why, instead of going home from the Railway Station, Mr. Anderson went to Captain Fraser's place he himself could not tell.

When the Andersons reached Captain Fraser's place at half past eight in the evening, Mr. and Mrs. Fraser had not come back from the club. But they were expected every minute. It was in fact nine when the Captain and his wife turned up in a Hackney Carriage. They were surprised to see the Andersons. They had heard the story told by Atkins at the club. Anderson gave them his version. Of course, Captain Fraser asked them to stay to dinner. He said "I am very sorry I am late, but it could not be helped. When returning from the club my horse was alarmed at something. The coachman lost control and there was a disaster. But, thank God, nobody is seriously hurt."

Their carriage had, however, been so badly damaged that they had to get a hackney carriage to bring them home.

In India, specially in June, they are not particular about the dress. So Captain Fraser said they would sit down to dinner at once and, at a quarter after nine they all went in to dine. The Khansama stared at the uninvited guests. He knew that something had gone wrong with Anderson Saheb.

The soup was the first thing brought in and the trouble began as soon as it came. Captain Fraser's Khansama was an old hand at his business, but somehow he made a mess of things. He got so nervous about what he himself could not explain that he upset a full plate of soup that he had brought for Mr. Anderson not exactly on his head, but on his left ear.

Well the reader would understand the situation. There was a plateful of hot soup on Mr. Anderson's left ear. The soup should have got cold, because it had waited long for the Captain's return from the club, but the cook had very prudently warmed it up again and it had become very warm indeed. Mr. Anderson shouted and the Khansama let go the plate. It fell on the table in front of Mr. Anderson on its edge and rolled on. Next to Mr. Anderson was Mrs. Fraser, and there was a glass of iced-water in front of her. The rolling soup plate upset the glass, and the water and the glass and the plate all came down on Mrs. Fraser's lap, the iced-water making her wet through and through. She was putting on a muslin gown. She had to go and change. Mrs. Anderson at this point got up and said that they would not spoil the Frasers' dinner by their presence. She said that the curse of the Indian Fakir was on them and if they stayed the Frasers would have to go without dinner. Naturally she anticipated that some further difficulty would arise there when the next dish was brought in. The Frasers protested loudly but she dragged Mr. Anderson away. She had forgotten that she had had her lunch and her husband had not.

While going in their motor car from Mr. Fraser's house to their own they had to pass a bazaar on the way. In the bazar there was a sweetmeat shop. Mr. Anderson, whose condition could be better imagined than described asked his chauffeur to stop at the sweetmeat shop. It was a native shop with a fat native proprietor sitting without any covering upon his body on a low stool. As soon as he saw Mr. Anderson and his wife he rushed out of his shop with joined palms to enquire what the gentleman wanted. Mr. Anderson was evidently very popular with the native tradesmen and shop-keepers.

This shop-keeper had special reason to know Mr. Anderson, as it was the latter's custom to give a dinner to all his native workmen on Her Majesty's birthday, and this particular sweetmeat vendor used to get the contract for the catering. The birthday used to be observed in India on the 24th May and it was hardly a fortnight that this man had received a cheque for a pretty large amount from Mr. Anderson, for having supplied Mr. Anderson's native workmen with sweets.

Naturally he rushed out of his shop in that humble attitude. But in doing so he upset a whole dishful of sweets, and the big dish with the sweets went into the road-side drain. All the same the man came up and wanted to know the pleasure of the Saheb. Mr. Anderson told him that he was very hungry and wanted something to eat. "Certainly, Huzoor" said the Halwâi (Indian Confectioner) and fussily rushed in. He brought out some native sweets in a "dona" (cup made of leaves) but as misfortune would have it Mr. Anderson could not eat anything.

There was any amount of petroleum in the sweets. How it got in there was a mystery. Mr. Anderson asked his chauffeur to proceed. For fear of hurting the feeling of this kind old Halwâi Mr. Anderson did not do anything then; but scarcely had the car gone 200 yards when the "dona" with its contents untouched was on the road.

Mr. Anderson reached home at about half past ten. He expected to find no dinner at home. But he was relieved to hear from his bearer that dinner was ready. He rushed into his bath-room, had a cold bath and within five minutes was ready for dinner in the dining-room.

But the dinner would not come. After waiting for about 15 minutes the bearer (butler and foot man combined) was dispatched to the kitchen to enquire what the matter was. The cook came with a sad look upon his face and informed him that the dinner had been ready since 8-30 as usual, but as the Saheb had not returned he had kept the food in the kitchen and come out leaving the kitchen-door open. Unfortunately Mr. Anderson's dogs had finished the dinner in his absence, probably thinking that the master was dining out. In a case like this the cook, who had been in Mr. Anderson's service for a long time, expected to hear some hard words; but Mr. Anderson only laughed loud and long. The cook suggested that he should prepare another dinner, but Mr. Anderson said that it would not be necessary that night. The chauffeur subsequently informed the cook that the master and his wife had dined at Captain Fraser's, and finished with sweets at Gopal Halwai's shop. This explained the master's mirth to the cook's satisfaction.

What happened the next day to Mr. Anderson need not be told. It is too painful and too dirty a story. The fact remains that Mr. Anderson had no solid food the next day either. He thought he should die of starvation. He did not know how much longer the curse was going to last, or what else was in store for him.

On the morning of the third day the bearer came and reported that a certain Indian Fakir had invited Mr. Anderson to go and breakfast with him. How eagerly husband and wife went! The Fakir lived in a miserable hut on the bank of the river. He invited the couple inside his hut and gave them bread and water. Here was clean healthy looking bread after all, and Mr. Anderson never counted how many loaves he ate. But he had never eaten food with greater relish and pleasure in his life before. After the meal the Fakir who evidently knew Mr. Anderson said: "Saheb, you are a great man and a good man too. You are rich and you think that riches can purchase everything. You are wrong. The Giver of all things may turn gold into dust and gold may, by His order, lose all its purchasing capacity. This you have seen during the last two days. You have annoyed a man who has no gold but who has power. You think that the Deputy Commissioner has power—but he has not. The Deputy Commissioner gets his power from the King. The man whom you have offended got his power from the King of Kings."

"It is His pleasure that you should leave the station. The sooner you leave this place Saheb the better for you or you will starve. You can stay as long as you like here—but you will eat no food outside this hut of mine—you can try.

"You can go now and come back for your dinner when you require it—."

Mr. Anderson came back to the Fakir's cottage for his dinner, with his wife at nine in the evening.

Early, the next morning, he left the station and never came back.

Within a month he left India for good. The hospitable gentlemen of the station who had asked Mr. and Mrs. Anderson to have a meal with them will never forget the occasion.

This story, though it reads like a fairy tale, is nevertheless true. All the European gentlemen of J——knew it and if anyone of them happens to read these pages he will be able to certify that every detail is correct.

The Black Artist

In this connection it will not be out of place to mention some of the strange doings of the once famous Hasan Khan, the black artist of Calcutta. Fifty years ago there was not an adult in Calcutta who did not know his name and had not seen or at least heard of his marvellous feats.

I have heard any number of wonderful stories but I shall mention only two here which, though evidently not free from exaggeration, will give an idea of what the people came to regard him as capable of achieving, and also of the powers and attributes which he used to arrogate to himself. What happened was this.

There was a big reception in Government House at Calcutta. Now a native of Calcutta of those days knew what such a reception meant.

All public roads within half a mile of Government House were closed to wheeled and fast traffic.

The large compound was decorated with lamps and Chinese Lanterns in a manner that baffled description. Thousands of these Chinese Lanterns hung from the trees and twinkled among the foliage like so many coloured fireflies. The drives from the gates to the building had rows of these coloured lanterns on both sides; besides, there were coloured flags and Union Jacks flying from the tops of the poles, round which were coiled wreaths of flowers, and which also served to support the ropes or wires from which these lanterns were suspended.

The main building itself was illuminated with hundreds of thousands of candles or lamps and looked from a distance like a house on fire. From close quarters you could read "Long live the Queen" written in letters of fire on the parapets of the building, and could see the procession of carriages that passed up and down the drives so artistically decorated, and wonder that the spirited horses did not bolt or shy or kick over the traces when entering those lanes of fire.

There were no electric lights then in Calcutta or in any part of India, no motor cars and no rubber-tyred carriages.

On a reception night lots of people come to watch the decorations of Government House. Now-a-days Government House is illuminated with electricity; but I am told by my elders that in those days when tallow candles and tiny glass lamps were the only means of illumination the thing looked more beautiful and gorgeous.

The people who come to see the illumination pass along the road and are not allowed to stop. The law is that they must walk on and if a young child stops for more than half a minute his guardian, friend, nurse or companion is at once reminded by the policeman on duty that he or she must walk on; and these policemen of Calcutta, unlike the policemen of London, are not at all courteous in their manner or speech.

So it happened on a certain reception night that Hasan Khan the black artist went to see the decorations and while lingering on the road was rudely told by the policeman on duty to get away.

Ordinarily Hasan Khan was a man of placid disposition and polite manners. He told the policeman that he should not have been rude to a rate-payer who had only come to enjoy the glorious sight and meant no harm. He also dropped a hint that if the head of the police department knew that a subordinate of his was insulting Hasan Khan it would go hard with that subordinate.

This infuriated the policeman who blew his whistle which had the effect of bringing half a dozen other constables on the spot. They then gave poor Hasan Khan a thrashing and reported him to the Inspector on duty. As chance would have it this Inspector had not heard of Hasan Khan before. So he ordered that he should be detained in custody and charged next morning with having assaulted a public officer in the discharge of his duty.

The Inspector also received a warning but he did not listen to it. Then Hasan Khan took out a piece of paper and a pencil from his pocket and wrote down the number of each of the six or seven policemen who had taken part in beating him; and he assured everybody (a large number of persons had gathered now) present that the constables and the Inspector would be dismissed from Government service within the next one hour.

Most of the people had not seen him before and not knowing who he was, laughed. The Inspector and the constables laughed too. After the mirth had subsided Hasan Khan was ordered to be handcuffed and removed. When the handcuffs had been clapped on he smiled serenely and said "I order that all the lights within half a mile of where we are standing be put out at once." Within a couple of seconds the whole place was in darkness.

The entire Government House Compound which was

a mass of fire only a minute before was in total darkness and the street lamps had gone out too. The only light that remained was on the street lamp-post under which our friends were.

The commotion at the reception could be more easily imagined than described.

There was total darkness everywhere. The guests were treading literally on each other's toes and the accidents that happened to the carriages and horses were innumerable.

As good luck would have it another Police Inspector who was also on duty and was on horse-back came up to the only light within a circle of half a mile radius.

To him Hasan Khan said "Go and tell your Commissioner of Police that his subordinates have ill-treated Hasan Khan and tell him that I order him to come here at once."

Some laughed others scoffed but the Inspector on horse-back went and within ten minutes the Commissioner of the Calcutta Police came along with half a dozen other high officials enquiring what the trouble was about.

To them Hasan Khan told the story of the thrashing he had received and pointed out the assailants. He then told the Commissioner that if those constables and the Inspector who had ordered him to be handcuffed were dismissed, on the spot, from Government service, the lamps would be lighted without human assistance.

To the utter surprise of everybody present (including the high officials who had come out with the Commissioner of Policc) an order dismissing the constables and the Inspector was passed and signed by the Commissioner in the dim light shed by that isolated lamp; and within one second of the order the entire compound of Government

House was lighted up again, as if some one had switched on a thousand electric lamps controlled by a single button.

Everybody who was present there enjoyed the whole thing excessively, with the exception of the police officers who had been dismissed from service.

It appeared that the Commissioner of Police knew a lot about Hasan Khan and his black art. How he had come to know of Hasan Khan's powers will now be related.

Most of my readers have heard the name of Messrs. Hamilton and Co., Jewellers of Calcutta. They are the oldest and most respectable firm of Jewellers probably in the whole of India.

One day Hasan Khan walked into their shop and asked to see some rings.

He was shown a number of rings but he particularly approved a cheap ring set with a single ruby. The price demanded for this ring was too much for poor honest Hasan Khan's purse, so he proposed that the Jewellers should let him have the ring on loan for a month.

This, of course, the Jewellers refused to do and in a most un-Englishman-like and unbusiness-like manner a young shop assistant asked him to clear out.

He promptly walked out of the shop promising to come again the next day. Before going out of the shop, however, he told one of the managers that the young shop assistant had been very rude to him and would not let him have the ring for a month.

The next day there was a slight commotion in Hamilton's shop. The ring was missing. Of course, nobody could suspect Hasan Khan because the ring had been seen by everybody in the shop after his departure. The police were communicated with and were soon on the spot. They were examining the room and the locks and recording statements when Hasan Khan walked in with the missing ring on his finger.

He was at once arrested, charged with theft and taken to the police station and locked up.

At about midday he was produced before the Magistrate. When he appeared in court he was found wearing ten rings, one on each finger. He was remanded and taken back to his cell in the jail.

The next morning when the door of his cell was opened it was found that one of the big almirahs in which some gold and silver articles were kept in Hamilton's shop was standing in his cell. Everybody gazed at it dumbfounded. The almirah with its contents must have weighed 50 stones. How it got into the cell was beyond comprehension.

All the big officers of Government came to see the fun and asked Hasan Khan how he had managed it.

"How did you manage to get the show-case in your drawing-room?" inquired Hasan Khan of each officer in reply to the question.

And everybody thought that the fellow was mad. But as each officer reached home he found that one show-case (evidently from Hamilton's shop) with all its contents was standing in his drawing room.

The next morning Hasan Khan gave out in clear terms that unless Messrs. Hamilton and Co. withdrew the charge against him at once they would find their safe in which were kept the extra valuable articles, at the bottom of the Bay of Bengal.

The Jewellers thought that prudence was the best part of valour and the case against Hasan Khan was withdrawn and he was acquitted of all charges and set at liberty.

Then arose the big question of compensating him for the incarceration he had suffered; and the ring with the single ruby which he had fancied so much and which had caused all this trouble was presented to him.

Of course, Messrs. Hamilton and Co. the Jewellers, had to spend a lot of money in carting back the show-cases that had so mysteriously walked away from their shop, but they were not sorry, because they could not have advertised their ware better, and everybody was anxious to possess something or other from among the contents of these peculiar show-cases.

It was in connection with this case that Hasan Khan became known to most of the European Government officials of Calcutta at that time.

The Bridal Party

In Benares, the sacred city of the Hindus, situated in the United Provinces of Agra and Oudh, there is a house which is famed pretty far and wide. It is said that the house is haunted and that no human being can pass a night in that house.

Once there was a large Bridal party.

In India the custom is that the bridegroom goes to the house of the bride with great pomp and show with a number of friends and followers and the ceremony of "Kanya Dan" (giving away the girl) takes place at the bride's house.

The number of the people who go with the bridegroom depends largely upon the means of the bride's party, because the guests who come with the groom are to be fed and entertained in right regal style. It is this feeding and entertaining the guests that makes a daughter's marriage so costly in India, to a certain extent.

If the bride and the bridegroom live in the same town or village then the bridegroom's party goes to the bride's house in the evening, the marriage is performed at night and they all come away the same night or early the next morning. If, however, the places of residence of the bride and the bridegroom are say 500 miles apart as is generally the case, the bridegroom with his party goes a day or two earlier and stays a day or two after the marriage. The bride's people have to find accommodation, food and entertainment for the whole period, which in the case of rich people extends over a week.

Now I had the pleasure of joining such a bridal party as mentioned last, going to Benares.

We were about thirty young men, besides a number of elderly people.

Since the young men could not be merry in the presence of their elders the bride's father, who was a very rich man, had made arrangements to put up the thirty of us in a separate house. This house was within a few yards of the famed haunted house.

We reached Benares at about ten in the morning and it was about three in the afternoon that we were informed that the celebrated haunted house was close by. Naturally some of us decided that we should occupy that house rather than the one in which we were. I myself was not very keen on shifting but a few others were. Our host protested but we insisted, and so the host had to give way.

The house was empty and the owner was a local gentleman, a resident of Benares.

To procure his permission and the key was the work of a few minutes and we took actual possession of the house at about six in the evening. It was a very large house with big rooms and halls (rather poorly furnished) but some furniture was brought in from the house which we had occupied on our arrival.

There was a very big and well-ventilated hall and in this we decided to sleep. Carpet upon carpet was piled on the floor and there we decided to sleep (on the ground) in right Oriental style. Lamps were brought and the house was lighted up.

The Bridal Party

At about 9 P.M. our dinner was announced. The Oriental dinner is conducted as follows:—

The guests all sit on the floor and a big plate of metal (say 20" in diameter) is placed in front of each guest. Then the service commences and the plates are filled with dainties. Each guest generally gets thrice as much as he can eat. Then the host who does not himself join stands with joined hands and requests the guests to do full justice, and the dinner begins. Very little is eaten in fact, and whatever is left goes to the poor. That is probably the only consolation. Now on this particular occasion the bride's father, who was our host and who was an elderly gentleman had withdrawn, leaving two of his sons to look after us. He himself, we understood, was looking after his more elderly guests who had been lodged in a different house.

The hall in which we sat down to dine was a large one and very well lighted.

Adjoining it was the hall in which our beds had been made. The sons of mine host with a number of others were serving. I always was rather unconventional. So I asked my fellow guests whether I could fall to, and without waiting for permission I commenced eating, a very good thing I did, as would appear hereafter.

In about 20 minutes the serving was over and we were asked to begin. As a matter of fact I was nearly half through at that time. And then the trouble began.

With a click all the lights went out and the whole house was in total darkness.

Of course, the reader can guess what followed.

"Who has put out the lights?" shouted Jagat, who was sitting next but one to me on the left.

"The ghost" shouted another in reply.

"I shall kill him if I can catch him" shouted Jagat.

The whole place was in darkness, we could not see anything but we could hear that Jagat was trying to get up.

Then he received what was a stunning blow on his back. We could hear the thump.

"Oh" shouted Jagat "who is that?"

He sat down again and gave the man on his right a blow like the one he had received. The man on the right protested. Then Jagat turned to the man on his left. The man on Jagat's left evidently resisted and Jagat had the worst of it.

Then Narain, another one of us shouted out.

"What is the matter with you?" asked his neighbour.

"Why did you pull my hair" shouted Narain.

"I did not pull" shouted the neighbour.

Then a servant was seen approaching with a lamp and things became quiet.

But the servant did not reach the hall. He stumbled against something and fell headlong on the ground, the lamp went out, and our trouble began again.

One of the party received a slap on the back of his head which sent his cap rolling and in his attempt to recover it he upset a glass of water that was near his right hand.

Matters went on in this fashion till a lamp came. The whole thing must have taken about 4 minutes. When the lamp came we found that all the dishes were clean.

The eatables had mysteriously disappeared.

The sons of mine host looked stupidly at us and we looked stupidly at them and at each other. But there it was, there was not a particle of solid food left.

We had therefore no alternative but to adjourn to the nearest confectioner's shop and eat some sweets there. That the night would not pass in peace we were sure; but nobody dared suggest that we should not pass the night in the haunted house. Once having defied the Ghost we had to stand to our guns for one night at least.

It was well after 11 o'clock at night when we came back and went to bed. We went to bed but not to sleep.

The room in which we all slept was a big one as I have said already, and there were two wall lamps in it. We lowered the lamps and—

Then the lamps went out, and we began to anticipate trouble. Our hosts had all gone home leaving us to the tender mercies of the Ghost.

Shortly afterwards we began to feel as if we were lying on a public road and horses passing along the road within a yard of us. We also imagined we could hear men passing close to us whispering. Sleeping was impossible. We all remained awake talking about different things, till a horse came very near. And thus the night passed away. At about four in the morning one of us got up and wanted to go out.

We shouted for the servant called Kallu and within a minute Kallu came with a lantern. One of our fellow guests got up and went out of the room followed by Kallu.

We could hear him going along the dining hall to the head of the stairs. Then we heard him shriek. We all rushed out. The lighted lantern was there at the head of the stairs and our fellow guest at the bottom. Kallu had vanished.

We rushed down, picked up our friend and carried him upstairs. He said that Kallu had given him a push and he had fallen down. Fortunately he was not hurt. We called the servants and they all came, Kallu among them. He denied having come with a lantern or having pushed our friend down the stairs. The other servants corroborated his statement. They assured us that Kallu had never left the room in which they all were.

We were satisfied that this was also a ghostly trick.

At about seven in the morning when our hosts came we were glad to bid good-bye to the haunted house with our bones whole.

The funniest thing was that only those of my fellow guests had the worst of it who had denied the existence of Ghosts. Those of us who had kept respectfully silent had not been touched.

Those who had received a blow or two averred that the blows could not have been given by invisible hands inasmuch as the blows were too substantial. But all of us were certain that it was no trick played by a human being.

The passing horses and the whispering passers-by had given us a queer creepy sensation.

The Governor General's House

Here is the story of a well-known haunted houses in Calcutta.

The "Hastings House" is situated at Alipore in the Southern suburb of Calcutta. This is a big palatial building now owned by the Government of Bengal. At one time it was the private residence of the Governor-General of India whose name it bears. At present it is used as the "State Guest House" in which the Indian Chiefs are put up when they come to pay official visits to His Excellency in Calcutta. It appears that in a lane not very far from this house was fought the celebrated duel between Warren Hastings, the first Governor-General of India and Sir Philip Francis, a Member of his Council and the reputed author of the "Letters of Junius."

While living in this house Warren Hastings married Baroness Imhoff sometime during the first fortnight of August about 140 years ago. "The event was celebrated by great festivities"; and, as expected, the bride came home in a splendid equipage. It is said that this scene is re-enacted on the anniversary of the wedding by supernatural agency and a ghostly carriage duly enters the gate in the evening once every year. The clatter of hoofs and the rattle of iron-tyred wheels are distinctly heard advancing up to the portico; then there is the sound of the opening and closing of the carriage door, and lastly the carriage proceeds onwards, but it does not come out from under the porch. It vanishes mysteriously.

To-day is the 15th of August and this famous equipage must have glided in and out to the utter bewilderment of watchful eyes and ears within the last fortnight.

NOTE: Since the publication of the first edition "Hasting House" has been converted into an Indian Rugby for the benefit of the cadets of the rich families in Bengal.

Open Windows

Here is another tale of a well-known ghostly house in Calcutta in which the only trouble is that its windows in the first floor bedrooms open at night spontaneously.

People have slept at night for a reward in this house closing the windows with their own hands and have waked up at night shivering with cold to find all the windows open.

Once a body of soldiers went to pass a night in this house with a view to solve the mystery. They all sat in a room fully determined not to sleep but see what happened; and thus went on chatting till it was about midnight. There was a big lamp burning on a table around which they were seated. All of a sudden there was a loud click—the lamp went out and all the windows opened simultaneously. The next minute the lamp was alight again. The occupants of the room looked at their watches; it was about 1 A.M. The next night they sat up again and one of them with a revolver. At about one in the morning this particular individual pointed his revolver at one of the windows. As soon as the lamp went out this man pulled the trigger five times and there were five reports. The windows, however, opened and the lamp was alight again as on the previous night. They all rushed to the window to see if any damage had been done by the bullets.

The five bullets were found in the room but from their appearance it seemed as if they had struck nothing, evidently the bullets would have been changed in shape if they had impinged upon any hard substance. But then this was another enigma. How did the bullets come back? No man could have put the bullets there from before, (for they were still hot when discovered) or could have guessed the bore of the revolver that was going to be used.

On the third night to make assurance doubly sure, these soldiers were again present in the room, but on this occasion they had loaded their revolver with marked bullets.

As it neared one o'clock, one of them pointed the revolver at the window. He had decided to pull the trigger as soon as the lamp would go out. But he could not. As soon as the lamp went out this soldier received a sharp cut on his wrist with a cane and the revolver fell clattering on the floor. The invisible hand had left its mark behind which his companions saw after the lamp was alight again.

Many people have subsequently tried to solve the mystery but never succeeded.

The house remained untenanted for a long time and finally it was rented by an Australian horse dealer who however did not venture to occupy the building itself, and contented himself with erecting his stables and offices in the compound where he is not molested by the unearthly visitors.

You Will Like to Kiss It

This is a story of another ghostly house in an unnamed town in the United Provinces. It is said that various people saw numerous things in that house but a correct report never came. Once a friend of mine passed a night in that house. He told me what he had seen. Most wonderful! This is his story and I have no reason to disbelieve him.

"I went to pass a night in that house and I had only a comfortable chair, a small table and a few magazines besides a loaded revolver. I had taken care to load that revolver myself so that there might be no trick and I had given everybody to understand that.

"I began well. The night was cool and pleasant. The lamp bright—the chair comfortable and the magazine which I took up—interesting.

"But at about midnight I began to feel rather uneasy.

"At one in the morning I should probably have left the place if I had not been afraid of friends whose servants I knew were watching the house and its front door.

"At half past one I heard a peculiar sigh of pain in the next room. 'This is rather interesting,' I thought. To face something tangible is comparatively easy; to wait for the unknown is much more difficult. I took out the revolver from my pocket and examined it. It looked quite all right—this small piece of metal which could have killed six men in half a minute. Then I waited—for what—well.

"A couple of minutes of suspense and the sigh was repeated. I went to the door dividing the two rooms and pushed it open. A long thick ray of light at once penetrated the darkness, and I walked into the other room. It was only partially light. But after a minute I could see all the corners. There was nothing in that room.

"I waited for a minute or two. Then I heard the sigh in the room which I had left. I came back,—stopped—rubbed my eyes—.

"Sitting in the chair which I had vacated not two minutes ago was a young girl calm, fair, beautiful with that painful expression on her face which could be more easily imagined than described. I had heard of her. So many others who had came to pass a night in that house had seen her and described her (and I had disbelieved).

"Well—there she sat, calm, sad, beautiful, in my chair. If I had come in five minutes later I might have found her reading the magazine which I had left open, face downwards. When I was well within the room she stood up facing me and I stopped. The revolver fell from my hand. She smiled a sad sweet smile. How beautiful she was!

"Then she spoke. A modern ghost speaking like Hamlet's father, just think of that!

"'You will probably wonder why I am here—I shall tell you, I was murdered—by my own father.... I was a young widow living in this house which belonged to my father I became unchaste and to save his own name he poisoned me when I was *enceinte*—another week and I should have become a mother; but he poisoned me and my innocent child died too—it would have been such a beautiful baby—and you would probably want to kiss it'

and horror of horrors, she took out the child from her womb and showed it to me. She began to move in my direction with the child in her arms saying—'You will like to kiss it.'

"I don't know whether I shouted—but I fainted.

"When I recovered consciousness it was broad day-light, and I was lying on the floor, with the revolver by my side. I picked it up and slowly walked out of the house with as much dignity as I could command. At the door I met one of my friends to whom I told a lie that I had seen nothing.—It is the first time that I have told you what I saw at the place.

"The Ghostly woman spoke the language of the part of the country in which the Ghostly house is situate."

The friend who told me this story is a responsible Government official and will not make a wrong statement. What has been written above has been confirmed by others—who had passed nights in that Ghostly house; but they had generally shouted for help and fainted at the sight of the ghost, and so they had not heard her story from her lips as reproduced here.

The house still exists, but it is now a dilapidated old affair, and the roof and the doors and windows are so bad that people don't care to go and pass a night there.

There is also a haunted house in Assam. In this house a certain gentleman committed suicide by cutting his own throat with a razor.

You often see him sitting on a cot in the verandah heaving deep sighs.

Mention of this house has been made in a book called *Tales from the Tiger Land* published in England. The Author says he has passed a night in the house in question and testifies to the accuracy of all the rumours that are current.

The Haunted Tank

This is the tale of a haunted tank at the house of a friend of mine.

I was visiting a friend of mine in the interior of Bengal during our annual summer holidays when I was yet a student. This friend of mine was the son of a rich man and in the village had a large ancestral house where his people usually resided. It was the first week of June when I reached my friend's house. I was informed that among other things of interest, which were, however, very few in that particular part of the country, there was a large Pukka tank belonging to my friend's people which was haunted.

What kind of Ghost lived in the tank or near it nobody could say, but what everybody knew was this, that on Jaistha Shukla Ekadashi (that is on the eleventh day after the new moon in the month of Jaistha) that occurs about the middle of June, the Ghost comes to bathe in the tank at about midnight.

Of course, Jaistha Shukla Ekadashi was only 3 days off, and I decided to prolong my stay at my friend's place, so that I too might have a look at the Ghost's bath.

On the eventful day I resolved to pass the night with my friend and two other intrepid souls, near the tank.

After a rather late dinner, we started with a bedding and a Hookah and a pack of cards and a big lamp. We made the bed (a mattress and a sheet) on a platform on the bank. There were six steps, with risers about 9" each, leading from the platform to the water. Thus we were about 4½ feet from the water level; and from this coign of vantage we could command a full view of the tank, which covered an area of about four acres. Then we began our game of cards. There was a servant with us who was preparing our Hookah.

At midnight we felt we could play no longer.

The strain was too great; the interest too intense.

We sat smoking and chatting and asked the servant to remove the lamp as a lot of insects was coming near attracted by the light. As a matter of fact we did not require any light because there was a brilliant moon. At one o'clock in the morning there was a noise as of rushing wind—we looked round and found that not a leaf was moving but still the whizzing noise as of a strong wind continued. Then we found something advancing towards the tank from the opposite bank. There was a number of cocoanut trees on the bank on the other side, and in the moonlight we could not see clearly what it really was. It looked like a huge white elephant. It approached the tank at a rapid pace—say the pace of a fast trotting horse. From the bank it took a long leap and with a tremendous splash fell into the water. The plunge made the water rise on our side and it rose as high as 4½ feet because we got wet through and through.

The mattress and the sheet and all our clothes were wet. In the confusion we forgot to keep our eyes on the Ghost or white elephant or whatever it was and when we again looked in that direction everything was quiet. The apparition had vanished.

The most wonderful thing was the rise in the water level.

For the water to rise 4½ feet would have been impossible under ordinary circumstances even if a thousand elephants had got into the water.

We were all wide awake—We went home immediately because we required a change of clothes.

The old man (my friend's father) was waiting for us. "Well you are wet" he said.

"Yes" said we.

"Rightly served" said the old man.

He did not ask what had happened. We were told subsequently that he had got wet like us a number of times when he was a youngster himself.

A Strange Incident

When I was at college there happened what was a most inexplicable incident.

The matter attracted some attention at that time, but has now been forgotten as it was really not so very extraordinary. The police in fact, when called in, explained the matter or at least thought they had done so, to everybody's satisfaction. I was, however, not satisfied with the explanation given by the police. This was what actually happened.

The college was a very big one with a large boarding-house attached to it. The boarding-house was a building separate from the college situated at a distance of about 100 yards from the college building. It was in the form of a quadrangle with a lawn in the centre. The area of this lawn must have been 2,500 square yards. Of course it was surrounded on all sides by buildings, that is, by a row of single rooms on each side.

In the boarding-house there was a common room for the amusement of the students. There were all sorts of indoor games including a miniature billiard table in this common room. I was a regular visitor there. I did not care for any other indoor game than chess. Of course chess meant keeping out of bed, till late at night.

On this particular occasion, I think it was in November,

a certain gentleman, who was an ex-student of the college, was paying us a visit. He was staying with us in the boarding-house. He had himself passed 4 years in that boarding-house and naturally had a love for it. In his time he was very popular with the other boarders and with the Superintendent. Dr. M.N., an English gentleman who was also an inmate of the Boarding-House. With the permission of the learned Doctor, the Superintendent, we decided to make a night of it, and so we all assembled in the common room after dinner. I can picture to myself the cheerful faces of all the students present on that occasion in the well lighted Hall. So far as I know only one of that group is now dead. He was the most jovial and the best beloved of all. May he rest in peace!

Now to return from this mournful digression. I could see old Mathura sitting next to me with a Hookah with a very long stem, directing the moves of the chessmen. There was old Birju at the miniature billiard table poking at everybody with his cue who laughed when he missed an easy shot.

Then came in the Superintendent, Dr. M.N. and in a hurry to conceal his Hookah (Indians never smoke in the presence of their elders and superiors) old Mathura nearly upset the table on which the chessmen were; and the mirth went on with redoubled vigour as the Doctor was one of the loudest and merriest of the whole lot on such occasions.

Thus we went on till nearly one in the morning when the Doctor ordered everybody to go to bed. Of course we were glad to retire but we were destined to be soon disturbed.

Earlier the same evening we had been playing a friendly

A Strange Incident

Hockey match, and one of the players, let us call him Ram Gholam, had been slightly hurt. As a matter of fact he always got hurt whenever he played.

During the evening the hurt had been forgotten but as soon as he was in bed it was found that he could not sleep. The matter was reported to the Superintendent who finding that there was really nothing the matter with him suggested that the affected parts should be washed with hot water and finally wrapped in heated castor leaves and bandaged over with flannel. (This is the best medicine for gouty pain—not for hurt caused by a hockey stick).

There was a castor tree in the compound and a servant was despatched to bring the leaves. In the meantime a few of us went to the kitchen, made a fire and boiled some water. While thus engaged we heard a noise and a cry for help. We rushed out and ran along the verandah (corridor) to the place whence the cry came. It was coming from the room of Prayag, one of the boarders. We pushed the door but found that it was bolted from inside, we shouted to him to open but he would not. The door had four glass panes on the top and we discovered that the upper bolt only had been used; as a matter of fact the lower bolts had all been removed, because on closing the door from outside, once it had been found that a bolt at the bottom had dropped into its socket and the door had to be broken before it could be opened.

Prayag's room was in darkness. There was a curtain inside and so we could see nothing from outside. We could hear Prayag groaning. The Superintendent came up. To break the glass pane nearest to the bolt was the work of a minute. The door was opened and we all rushed in. It was a room 14'x12'; many of us could not, therefore, come in. When we went in we took a light with us. It was one of the hurricane lanterns—the one we had taken to the kitchen. The lamp suddenly went out. At the same time a brickbat came rattling down from the roof and fell near my feet, thus I could feel it with my feet and tell what it was. And Prayag groaned again. Dr. M.N. came in, and we helped Prayag out of his bed and took him out on the verandah. Then we saw another brickbat come from the roof of the verandah, and fell in front of Prayag a few inches from his feet. We took him to the central lawn and stood in the middle of it. This time a whole solid brick came from the sky. It fell a few inches from my feet and remained standing on its edge. If it had toppled over it would have fallen on my toes.

By this time all the boarders had come up. Prayag stood in the middle of the group shivering and sweating. A few more brickbats came but not one of us was hurt. Then the trouble ceased. We removed Prayag to the Superintendent's room and put him in the Doctor's bed. There were a reading lamp on a stool near the head of the bed and a Holy Bible on it. The learned Doctor must have been reading it when he was disturbed. Another bed was brought in and the Doctor passed the night in it.

In the morning came the police.

They found a goodly heap of brickbats and bones in Prayag's room and on the lawn. There was an investigation, but nothing came out of it. The police however explained the matter as follows:—

There were some people living in the two-storied houses in the neighbourhood. The brickbats and the bones must have come from there. As a matter of fact the police discovered that the Boarding House students and the people who lived in these houses were not on good terms. Those

A Strange Incident

people had organized a music party and the students had objected to it. The matter had been reported to the Magistrate and had ended in a decision in favour of the students. Hence the strained relations. This was the most natural explanation and the only explanation. But this explanation did not satisfy me for several reasons.

The first reason was that the college compound contained another well kept lawn that stood between the Hostel buildings and those two-storied houses. There were no brickbats on this lawn. If brickbats had been thrown from those houses some at least would have fallen upon the lawn.

Then as regarded the brickbats that were in the room, they had all dropped from the ceiling; but in the morning we found the tiles of the roof intact. Thirdly, in the middle of the central lawn there was at least one whole brick. The nearest building from which a brick might have been thrown was at a distance of 100 yards and to throw a whole brick 9"x4½"x3" such a distance would require a machine of some kind or other and none was found in the house.

The last thing that created doubts in my mind was this that not one brickbat had hit anybody. There were so many of us there and there was such an abundance of brickbats still not one of us was hit, and it is well known that brickbats hurled by Ghostly hands do not hit anybody. In fact the whole brick that came and stood on edge within 3 inches of my toe would have hurt me if it had only toppled over.

A Suttee Story

It is known to most of the readers that Sutteeism was the practice of burning the widows on the funeral pyre of their dead husbands. This practice was prevalent in Bengal down to the year 1828 when a law forbidding the aiding and abetting of Sutteeism was passed. Before the Act, of course, many women were, in a way, forced to become Suttees. The public opinion against a widow's surviving was so great that she preferred to die rather than live after her husband's death.

The law has, however, changed the custom and the public opinion too.

Still, every now and then there are found cases of determined Sutteeism among all classes in India who profess Hinduism. Frequent instances are found in Bengal; and whenever a case comes to the notice of the public the newspapers report it in a manner which shows that respect for the Suttee is not yet dead.

Sometimes a verdict of "Suicide during temporary insanity" is returned, but, of course, whoever reads the report understands how matters stand.

This story I heard recently, in which a gentleman who was in Government service died leaving a young widow.

A Suttee Story

When the husband's dead body was being removed the wife looked so jolly that nobody suspected that anything was wrong with her.

But when all the male members of the family had gone away with the bier the young widow quietly procured a tin of Kerosine oil and a few bed sheets. She soaked the bed sheets well in the oil and then wrapped them securely round her person and further secured them by means of a rope. She then shut all the doors of her room and set the clothes on fire. By the time the doors were forced open (there were only ladies in the house at that time) she was dead.

Of course this was a case of suicide pure and simple and there was the usual verdict of suicide during temporary insanity, but I personally doubt the temporary insanity very much. This case, however, is too painful.

The one that I am now going to relate is more interesting and more mysterious, and probably more instructive.

Babu Bhagwan Prasad, now the late Babu Bhagwan Prasad, was a clerk in the———office in the United Provinces. He was a grown-up man of 45 when the incident happened.

He had an attack of cold which subsequently developed into pneumonia and after a lingering illness of 8 days he died at about 8 o'clock one morning.

He had, of course, a wife and a number of children.

Babu Bhagwan Prasad was a well paid officer and maintained a large family consisting of brothers—their wives and their children.

At the time of his death, in fact, when the doctor went away in the morning giving his opinion that it was a question of minutes, his wife seemed the least affected of all. While all the members of the family were collected round the bed of their dying relative the lady withdrew to her room saying that she was going to dress for the journey. Of course nobody took any notice of her at the time. She retired to her room and dressed herself in the most elaborate style, and marked her forehead with a large quantity of "Sindur"* for the last time.

After dressing she came back to the room where her dying husband was and approached the bed. Those who were there made way for her in surprise. She sat down on the bed and finally lay down by her dying husband's side. This demonstration of sentimentalism could not be tolerated in a family where the Purda is strictly observed and one or two elderly ladies tried to remonstrate.

But on touching her they found that she was dead. The husband was dead too. They had both died simultaneously. When the doctor arrived he found the lady dead, but he could not ascertain the cause of her death.

Everybody thought she had taken poison but nothing could be discovered by post mortem examination.

There was not a trace of any kind of poison in the body.

The funeral of the husband and the wife took place that afternoon and they were cremated on the same pyre.

The stomach and some portions of the intestines of the deceased lady were sent to the chemical examiner and his report (which arrived a week later) did not disclose anything.

The matter remains a mystery.

It will never be found out what force killed the lady at such a critical moment. Probably it was the strong will of the Suttee that would not allow her body to be separated from that of her husband even in death.

---

*"Sindur" is red oxide of mercury or lead used by orthodox Hindu women in some parts of India whose husbands are alive; widows do not use it.

The Return of Smith

This story is said to come from a place near Agra in the United Provinces.

There were two respectable residents of the town who were close neighbours. For the convenience of the readers we shall call them Smith and Jones.

Smith and Jones, as has been said already, were close neighbours and the best of friends. Each had his wife and children living with him.

Now Mr. Smith got fever, on a certain very hot day in June. The fever would not leave him and on the tenth day it was discovered that it was typhoid fever of the worst type.

Now typhoid fever is in itself very dangerous, but more so in the case of a person who gets it in June. So poor Smith had no chance of recovery. Of course Jones knew it. Mrs. Smith was a rather uneducated elderly lady and the children were too young. So the medical treatment as well as the general management of Mr. Smith's affairs was left entirely in the hands of Mr. Jones.

Mr. Jones did his best. He procured the best medical advice. He got the best medicines prescribed by the doctors and engaged the best nurse available. But his efforts were of no avail. On a certain Thursday afternoon Smith began to sink fast and at about eight in the evening he died.

Mr. Jones on his return from his office that day at about

four in the afternoon had been informed that Mr. Smith's condition was very bad, and he had at once gone over to see what he could do.

He had sent for half a dozen doctors, but they on their arrival had found that the case was hopeless. Three of the doctors had accordingly gone away, but the other three had stayed behind.

When however Smith was dead, and these three doctors had satisfied themselves that life was quite extinct, they too went away with Mr. Jones leaving the dead body in charge of the mourning members of the family of the deceased.

Mr. Jones at once set about making arrangements for the funeral early the next morning; and it was well after eleven at night that he returned to a very late dinner at his own house. It was a particularly hot night and after smoking his last cigar for the day Mr. Jones went to bed, but not to sleep, after midnight. The death of his old friend and neighbour had made him very sad and thoughtful. The bed had been made on the open roof on the top of the house which was a two storied building and Mr. Jones lay watching the stars and thinking.

At about one in the morning there was a loud knock at the front door. Mr. Jones who was wide awake thought it was one of the servants returning home late and so he did not take any notice of it.

After a few moments the knock was repeated at the door which opened on the stairs leading to the roof of the second storey on which Mr. Jones was sleeping. [The visitor had evidently passed through the front door]. This time Mr. Jones knew it was no servant. His first impression was that it was one of the mutual friends who had heard of Smith's death and was coming to make enquiries. So he shouted out "Who is there?"

"It is I,—Smith" was the reply.

"Smith—Smith is dead" stammered Mr. Jones.

"I want to speak to you, Jones—open the door or I shall come and kill you" said the voice of Smith from beyond the door. A cold sweat stood on Mr. Jones's forehead. It was Smith speaking, there was no doubt of that,—Smith, whom he had seen expire before his very eyes five hours ago. Mr. Jones began to look for a weapon to defend himself.

There was nothing available except a rather heavy hammer which had been brought up an hour earlier that very night to fix a nail in the wall for hanging a lamp. Mr. Jones took this up and waited for the spirit of Smith at the head of the stairs.

The spirit passed through this closed door also. Though the staircase was in total darkness still Mr. Jones could see Smith coming up step by step.

Up and up came Smith and breathlessly Jones waited with the hammer in his hand. Now only three steps divided them.

"I shall kill you" hissed Smith. Mr. Jones aimed a blow with the hammer and hit Smith between the eyes. With a groan Smith fell down. Mr. Jones fainted.

A couple of hours later there was a great commotion at the house of Mr. Smith. The dead body had mysteriously disappeared.

The first thing they could think of was to go and inform Mr. Jones.

So one of the young sons of Smith came to Mr. Jones's house. The servant admitted him and told him where to find the master.

Young Smith knocked at the door leading to the staircase but got no reply. "After his watchful nights he is sleeping soundly" thought young Smith.

But then Jones must be awakened.

The whole household woke up but not Mr. Jones. One of the servants then procured a ladder and got upon the roof. Mr. Jones was not upon his bed nor under it either. The servant thought he would open the door leading to the staircase and admit the people who were standing outside beyond the door at the bottom of the stairs. There was a number of persons now at the door including Mrs. Jones, her children, servants and young Smith.

The servant stumbled upon something. It was dark but he knew it was the body of his master. He passed on but then he stumbled again. There was another human being in the way. "Who is this other?—probably a thief" thought the servant.

He opened the door and admitted the people who were outside. They had lights with them. As they came in it was found that the second body on the stairs two or three steps below the landing was the dead body of Smith while the body on the landing was the unconscious form of Mr. Jones.

Restoratives were applied and Jones came to his senses and then related the story that has been recorded above. A doctor was summoned and he found the wound caused by Jones's hammer on Smith's head. There was a deep cut but no blood had come out, therefore, it appeared that the wound must have been caused at least two or three hours after death.

The doctors never investigated whether death could have been caused by the blow given by the hammer. They thought there was no need of an investigation either, because they had left Smith quite dead at eight in the evening.

How Smith's dead body was spirited away and came to Jones's house has been a mystery which will probably never be solved.

Thinking over the matter recorded above the writer has come to the conclusion that probably a natural explanation might be given of the affair.

Taking however all the facts of the case as given above to be true (and there is no reason to suppose that they are not) the only explanation that could be given and in fact that was given by some of the sceptical minds of Agra at that time was as follows:—

> "Smith was dead. Jones was a very old friend of his. He was rather seriously affected. He must have, in an unconscious state of mind like a somnambulist, carried the dead body of Smith to his own house without being detected in the act. Then his own fevered imagination endowed Smith with the faculty of speech, dead though the latter was; and in a moment of—well—call it temporary insanity, if you please—he inflicted the wound on the forehead of Smith's dead body."

This was the only plausible explanation that could be given of the affair; but regard being had to the fact that Smith's dead body was lying in an upper storey of the house and that there was a number of servants between the death chamber and the main entrance to the house, the act of removing the dead body without their knowing it was a difficult task, nay utterly impracticable.

Over and above this it was not feasible to carry away even at night, the dead body along the road, which is a well frequented thoroughfare, without being observed by anybody.

Then there is the third fact that Jones was really not such a strong person that he could carry alone Smith's body that distance with ease.

Smith's dead body as recovered in Jones' house had bare feet; whether there was any dust on the feet, had not been observed by anybody; otherwise some light might have been thrown on this apparently miraculous incident.

What the Professor Saw

This story is not so painful as the one entitled "What Uncle Saw." How we wish that uncle had seen something else, but all the same how glad we are that uncle did not see what the professor saw. The professor is an M.A. of the University of Calcutta, in Chemistry, and is a Lecturer in a big college. This, of course, I only mention to show that this is not the invention of a foolish person. I shall now tell the story as I heard it from the professor.

"I was a professor of chemistry in a Calcutta college in the year 18—. One morning I received a letter from home informing me that my eldest brother was ill. It was a case of fever due to cold. Of course, a man does sometimes catch cold and get fever too. There was nothing extraordinary about that.

"In the evening I did not receive any further news. This meant that my brother was better, because in any other case they would have written.

"A number of friends came to my diggings in the evening and invited me to join their party then going to a theatre. They had reserved some seat but one of the party for whom a seat had been reserved was unavoidably detained and hence a vacant seat. The news of my brother's illness had made me a little sad, the theatre, I thought, would cheer me up. So I joined.

"We left the theatre at about one in the morning. Coming to my house along the now deserted but well-lighted "College Street" of Calcutta I saw from a distance a tall man walking to and fro on the pavement in front of the Senate Hall. When I approached nearer I found that it was my brother of whose illness I had heard in the morning. I was surprised.

"'What are you doing here—brother.' I asked.

"'I came to tell you something.'

"'But you were ill—I heard this morning—by what train did you come?' I asked.

"'I did not come by train—never mind—I went to your *basa* (lodgings) and found you were out—gone to the theatre, so I waited for you here as I thought you would prefer walking home instead of taking a hackney carriage—'

"'Very fortunate I did not take one—'

"'In that case I would have seen you at your quarters.'

"'Then come along with me—' I said.

"'No' he said 'I shall stay where I am—what I have come to tell you is this, that after I am gone you will take care of the mother and see that she has everything she wants—'

"'But where are you going—' I asked puzzled.

"'Never mind where I am going—but will you promise—'

"'Promise what—?' I asked.

"'That you will see that the mother has everything she wants.'

"'Certainly—but where on earth are you going—' I asked again.

"'I can depend upon your promise then' he said and vanished.

"He vanished mysteriously. In what direction he went

I could not say. There was no bye-lane near. It was a very well-lighted part of the city. He vanished into the thin air. I rubbed my eyes and looked round.

"A policeman was coming along. He was about 50 feet away.

"I inquired him if he had seen the gentleman who was talking to me.

"'Did you see the other gentleman, officer?' I asked.

"'Yes' he said looking around 'there were two of you—where is the other—has he robbed you of all you had—these pickpockets have a mysterious way of disappearing—'

"'He was my brother' I said 'and no pickpocket.'

"The policeman looked puzzled too.

"I shouted aloud calling my brother by name but received no reply. I took out my gold watch. It was half past one. I walked home at a brisk pace.

"At home I was informed by the servant that my brother had come to look for me an hour ago but on being informed that I was out, had gone away.

"Whenever he came to Calcutta from the suburbs he put up with a friend of his instead of with me. So I decided to look him up at his friend's house in the morning. But I was not destined to carry out that plan.

"Early the next morning I received a telegram that my brother was dead. The telegram had been sent at 1.20 A.M. He must have died an hour before. Well—there it was.

"I had seen him and so had the policeman. The servant had seen him too. There could be no mistake about that.

"I took an early train and reached my suburban home at 10 A.M. I was informed that my brother had died at midnight. But I had seen him at about half past one and the servant had seen him at about 12.30. I did not tell anybody anything at that time. But I did so afterwards. I was not dreaming—because the conversation we had was a pretty long one. The servant and the police constable could not have been mistaken either. But the mystery remains."

This was the exact story of the professor. Here is something else to the point.

The Astral Lady & Others

Our next tale starts with a newspaper report......

Suicidal Telepathy

A remarkable case of what may be called suicidal telepathy has occurred near Geneva. Mme. Simon, a Swiss widow aged fifty, had been greatly distressed on account of the removal of her sister, who was five years younger, to a hospital. On Monday afternoon a number of persons who had ascended the Saleve, 4299 feet high, by the funicular railway, were horrified to see a woman walk out on to a ledge overlooking a sheer precipice of three hundred feet, and, after carefully wrapping a shawl round her head and face jump into space. The woman was Mme. Simon, says the Times of India, and she was found on the cliffs below in a mangled condition.

At the same time Mme. Simon's sister, who had not seen or communicated with the former for a week, became hysterical saying her sister was dead and that she did not want to survive her. During the temporary absence of the nurse the woman got out of her bed—opened the window and jumped into the road from the first floor. She is seriously injured and her recovery is doubtful.

The news of the death of Mme. Simon was only known at the hospital nine hours later.

The Leader
Allahabad, 12th February 1913.

Much more wonderful than all this is the story of "The Astral Lady" which appeared in one of the English Magazines a few months ago. In that case an English medical gentleman saw the Astral Lady in a first class railway compartment in England. Only accidentally he discovered the body of a lady nearly murdered and concealed under one of the seats. His medical help and artificial respiration and stimulants brought her round, and then the doctor saw the original of the Astral Lady in the recovered girl. Well—well—wonderful things do happen sometimes.

Mr. Justice Norman of the Calcutta High Court saw his mother while sitting in court one day and others saw her too. A few hours later his Lordship received a telegram informing him of her death at the moment when he had seen her in court. This was in broad daylight. Unlike the professor the judge did not even know that his mother was ill.

The fact that immediately after death the dead person appears to some one near and dear to him has been vouched for by others whose veracity and intelligence cannot be questioned.

The appearance of Miss Orme after her death at Mussoorie to Miss Mounce-Stephen in Lucknow was related in the Allahabad High Court during the trial of the latter lady for the murder of the former. This is on the record of the case. This case created a good deal of interest at the time.

Similar to what has been described above is the experience of Lord Brougham.

An extract from his memoirs is as follows:—

> "A most remarkable thing happened to me. So remarkable that I must tell the story from the beginning. After I left the High School (i.e. Edinburgh) I went with G—— my most intimate friend, to attend the classes of the University.
>
> "There was no divinity class, but we frequently in our walks discussed many grave subjects—among others— the Immortality of the soul and a future state. This question and the possibility of the dead appearing to the living were subjects of much speculation, and we actually committed the folly of drawing up an agreement, written with our blood, to the effect that whichever of us died the first should appear to the other and thus solve the doubts we had entertained of the life after death.
>
> "After we had finished our classes at the college, G—— went to India having got an appointment in the Civil Service there. He seldom wrote to me and after the lapse of a few years, I had nearly forgotten his existence. One day I had taken a warm bath, and, while lying in it enjoying the heat, I turned my head round, looking towards the chair on which I had deposited my clothes, as I was about to get out of the bath. On the chair sat G—looking calmly at me. How I got out of the bath I know

not, but on recovering my senses I found myself sprawling on the floor. The apparition or whatever it was that had taken the likeness of G—had disappeared. The vision had produced such a shock that I had no inclination to talk about it or to speak about it even to Stewart, but the impression it made upon me was too vivid to be forgotten easily, and so strongly was I affected by it that I have here written down the whole history with the date, 19th December, and all particulars as they are fresh before me now. No doubt I had fallen asleep and that the appearance presented so distinctly before my eyes was a dream I cannot doubt, yet for years I had no communication with G—nor had there been anything to recall him to my recollection. Nothing had taken place concerning our Swedish travel connected with G—or with India or with anything relating to him or to any member of his family. I recollected quickly enough our old discussion and the bargain we had made. I could not discharge from my mind the impression that G—— must have died and his appearance to me was to be received by me as a proof of a future state."

This was on the 19th December 1799.
In October 1862 Lord Brougham added a postscript.

"I have just been copying out from my journal the account of this strange dream.

"Certissima mortis imago, and now to finish the story begun about 60 years ago. Soon after my return to Edinburgh there arrived a letter from India announcing G's death, and that he died on the 19th December 1799."— *The Pall Mall Magazine* (1914) pp. 183-184.

Another very fine story and one to the point comes from Hyderabad.

A certain Mr. J—— who was an Englishman, after reading the memoirs of Lord Brougham, was so affected that he related the whole story to his confidential Indian servant. We need not mention here what Mr. J's profession was, all that we need say is that he was not very rich and in his profession there was no chance of his getting up one morning to find himself a millionaire.

The master and servant executed a bond written with their blood that he who died first would see the other a rich man.

As it happened the native servant died first, and on his death Mr. J—— who was then a young man retired altogether from his business, which business was not in a very flourishing condition. Within a couple of years he went to England a millionaire. How he came by his money remains a secret. People in England were told that he had earned it in India. He must have done so, but the process of his earning he has kept strictly to himself. Mr. J—— is still alive and quite hale.

On the Train & Others

A different event in which another friend of mine was concerned was thus described the other day.

He had received a telegram to the effect that a very near relation of his was dying in Calcutta and that this dying person was desirous to see him. He started for Calcutta in all haste by the mail. The mail used to leave his station at about 3 P.M. in the afternoon and reach Calcutta early the next morning. It was hot weather and in his first class compartment there was no other passenger. He lay down on one of the sleeping berths and the other one was empty. All the lamps including the night light had been switched off and the compartment was in total darkness, but for the moonlight. The moon beams too did not come into the compartment itself as the moon was nearly overhead.

He had fallen into a disturbed sleep when on waking up he found there was another occupant of the compartment. As thefts had been a common incident on the line specially in first class compartments, my friend switched on the electric light, the button of which was within his reach. This could be done without getting up.

In the glare of the electric light he saw distinctly his dying relation. He thought he was dreaming. He rubbed his eyes and then looked again. The apparition had vanished. He got up and looked out of the window. The train was passing through a station, without stopping. He could read the name of the station clearly. He opened his time table to see that he was still 148 miles from Calcutta.

Then he went to sleep again. In the morning he thought he had been dreaming. But he observed that the railway time table was still open at the place where he must have looked to ascertain the distance.

On reaching Calcutta he was told that his relation had died a few hours ago.

My friend never related this to anybody till he knew that I was writing on the subject. This story, however, after what the professor saw loses its interest; and some suggested that it had better not be written at all. I only write this because this friend of mine—who is also a relation of mine—is a big Government servant and would not have told this story unless it was true.

To the point is the following story which was in the papers about March 1914.

> 'In 1821 the Argyle Rooms were patronised by the best people, the establishment being then noted for high-class musical entertainments. One evening in March, 1821, a young Miss M. with a party of friends, was at a concert in Argyle Rooms. Suddenly she uttered a cry and hid her face in her hands. She appeared to be suffering so acutely that her friends at once left the building with her and took her home. It was at first difficult to get the young lady to explain the cause of her sudden attack, but at last she confessed that she had been terrified by a horrible sight. While the concert was in progress

she had happened to look down at the floor, and there lying at her feet she saw the corpse of a man. The body was covered with a cloth mantle, but the face was exposed, and she distinctly recognised the features of a friend, Sir J.T. On the following morning the family of the young lady received a message informing them that Sir J.T. had been drowned the previous day in Southampton Water through the capsizing of a boat, and that when his body was recovered it was entangled in a boat cloak. The story of the Argyle Rooms apparition is told by Mr. Thomas Raikes in his well-known diary, and he personally vouches for the truth of it.'

In this connection the following cutting from an English paper of March, 1914, will be found very interesting and instructive.

'Talks' With Mr. Stead
Sir A. Turner's Psychic Experiences

General Sir Alfred Turner's psychic experiences, which he related to the London Spiritualist Alliance on May 7, in the salon of the Royal Society of British Artists, cover a very wide field, and they date from his early boyhood.

The most interesting and suggestive relate to the re-appearance of Mr. Stead, says the Daily Chronicle. On the Sunday following the sinking of the Titanic, Sir Alfred was visiting a medium when she told him that on the glass of the picture behind his back the head of a man and afterwards 'its' whole form appeared. She described him minutely, and said he was holding a child by the hand. He had no doubt that it was Mr. Stead, and he wrote immediately to Miss Harper, Mr. Stead's private secretary. She replied saying that on the same day she had seen a similar apparition, in which Mr. Stead was holding a child by the hand.

A few days afterwards (continued Sir Alfred) at a private seance the voice of Stead came almost immediately and spoke at length. He told them what had happened in the last minutes of the wreck. All those who were on board when the vessel sank soon passed over, but they had not the slightest notion that they were dead. Stead knew however, and he set to work to try and tell these poor people that they had passed over and that there was at any rate no more physical suffering for them. Shortly afterwards he was joined by other spirits, who took part in the missionary work.

Mr. Stead was asked to show himself to the circle. He said 'Not now, but at Cambridge House.' At the meeting which took place there, not everybody was sympathetic, and the results were poor, except that Mr. Stead came to them in short sharp flashes dressed exactly as he was when on earth.

Since then, said Sir Alfred, he had seen and conversed with Mr. Stead many times. When he had shown himself he had said very little, when he did not appear he said a great deal.

On the occasion of his last appearance he said: 'I cannot speak to you. But pursue the truth. It is all truth.'

I am confident, Sir Alfred declared, that Mr. Stead will be of the greatest help to those of us who, on earth, work with him and to others who believe.

The Boy Possessed

This is a tale about a rich family in a great Indian city......

I think it was in 1906 that in one of the princial cities in India the son of a rich man became ill. He had high fever and delirium and in his insensible state he was constantly talking in a language which was some kind of English but which the relatives could not understand.

This boy was reading in one of the lower classes of a school and hardly knew the English language.

When the fever would not abate for 24 hours a doctor was sent for.

The doctor arrived, and went in to see the patient in the sick-room.

The boy was lying on the bed with his eyes closed. It was nearly evening.

As soon as the doctor entered the sick-room the boy shouted "Doctor—I am very hungry, order some food for me."

Of course, the doctor thought that the boy was in his senses. He did not know that the boy had not sufficient knowledge of the English language to express his ideas in that tongue. So the doctor asked his relations when he had taken food last. He was informed that the patient had had nothing to eat for the last 8 or 10 hours.

"What will you like to have?" asked the doctor.

"Roast mutton and plenty of vegetables" said the boy.

By this time the doctor had approached the bed-side, but it was too dark to see whether the eyes of the patient were open or not.

"But you are ill—roast mutton will do you harm" said the doctor.

"No it won't—I know what is good for me" said the patient. At this stage the doctor was informed that the patient did not really know much English and that he was probably in delirium. A suggestion was also made that probably he was possessed by a ghost.

The doctor who had been educated at the Calcutta Medical College did not quite believe the ghost theory. He, however, asked the patient who he was.

In India, I do not know whether this is so in European countries too, lots of people are possessed by ghosts and the ghost speaks through his victim. So generally a question like this is asked by the exorcist "Who are you and why are you troubling the poor patient?" The answer, I am told, is at once given and the ghost says what he wants. Of course, I personally, have never heard a ghost talk. I know a case in which a report was made to me that the wife of a groom of mine had become possessed by a ghost. On being asked what ghost it was the woman was reported to have said "the big ghost of the house across the drain." I ran to the out-houses to find out how much was true but when I reached the stables the woman I was told was not talking. I found her in convulsions.

To return to our story; the doctor asked the patient who he was.

"I am General——" said the boy.

"Why are you here" asked the doctor.

"I shall tell you that after I have had my roast mutton and the vegetables—" said the boy or rather the ghost.

"But how can we be convinced that you are General——" asked the doctor.

"Call Captain X—— of the XI Brahmans and he will know," said the ghost, "in the meantime get me the food or I shall kill the patient."

The father of the patient at once began to shout that he would get the mutton and the vegetables. The Doctor in the meantime rushed out to procure some more medical assistance as well as to fetch Captain X of the XI Brahmans.

The few big European officers of the station were also informed and within a couple of hours the sick-room was full of sensible educated gentlemen. The mutton was in the meantime ready.

"The mutton is ready" said the doctor.

"Lower it into the well in the compound" said the ghost.

A basket was procured and the mutton and the vegetables were lowered into the well.

But scarcely had the basket gone down 5 yards (the well was 40 feet deep) when somebody from inside the well shouted.

"Take it away—take it away—there is no salt in it."

Those that were responsible for the preparation had to admit their mistake.

The basket was pulled out, some salt was put in, and the basket was lowered down again.

But as the basket went in about 5 or 6 yards somebody from inside the well pulled it down with such force that the man who was lowering it narrowly escaped being dragged in; fortunately he let the rope slip through his hands with the result that though he did not fall into the well his hands were bleeding profusely.

Nothing happened after that and everybody returned to the patient.

After a few minutes silence the patient said:—

"Take away the rope and the basket, why did you not tie the end of the rope to the post."

"Why did you pull it so hard" said one of the persons present.

"I was hungry and in a hurry" said the ghost.

They asked several persons to go down into the well but nobody would. At last a fishing hook was lowered down. The basket, which had at first completely disappeared, was now floating on the surface of the water. It was brought up, quite empty.

Captain X in the meantime had arrived and was taken to the patient. Two high officials of Government (both Europeans) had also arrived.

As soon as the Captain stepped into the sick room the patient (we shall now call him the Ghost) said. "Good evening Captain X, these people will not believe that I am General—and I want to convince them."

The Captain was as surprised as the others had been before.

"You may ask me anything you like Captain X, and I shall try to convince you" said the Ghost.

The Captain stood staring.

"Speak, Captain X,—are you dumb?" said the Ghost.

"I don't understand anything" stammered the Captain.

He was told everything by those present. After hearing it the Captain formulated a question from one of the Military books.

A correct reply was immediately given. Then followed a number of questions by the Captain, the replies to all of which were promptly given by the Ghost.

After this the Ghost said, "If you are all convinced, you may go now, and see me again to-morrow morning."

Everybody quietly withdrew.

The next morning there was a large gathering in the sick room. A number of European officers who had heard the story at the club on the previous evening dropped in. "Introduce each of these new comers to me" said the Ghost.

Captain X introduced each person in solemn form.

"If anybody is curious to know anything I shall tell him" said the Ghost.

A few questions about England—position of buildings,—shops,—streets in London, were asked and correctly answered.

After all the questions the Indian Doctor who had been in attendance asked "Now, General, that we are convinced you are so and so why are you troubling this poor boy?"

"His father is rich" said the Ghost.

"Not very," said the doctor "but what do you want him to do?"

"My tomb at——pur has been destroyed by a branch of a tree falling upon it, I want that to be properly repaired" said the Ghost.

"I shall get that done immediately" said the father of the patient.

"If you do that within a week I shall trouble your boy no longer" said the Ghost.

The monument was repaired and the boy has been never ill since.

This is the whole story; a portion of it appeared in the

papers; and there were several respectable witnesses, though the whole thing is too wonderful.

Inexplicable as it is—it appears that dead persons are a bit jealous of the sanctity of their tombs.

The Burning

> I have heard a story of a boy troubled by a Ghost who had inscribed his name on the tomb of a Mahommedan fakir.

His father had to repair the tomb and had to put an ornamental iron railing round it.

Somehow or other the thing looks like a fairy tale. The readers may have heard stories like this themselves and thought them as mere idle gossip.

I, therefore, reproduce here the whole of a letter as it appeared in *The Leader* of Allahabad on the 15th July, 1913.

The letter is written by a man, who, I think, understands quite well what he is saying.

> Sir, It may probably interest your readers to read the account of a supernatural phenomenon that occurred, a few days ago, in the house of B. Rasiklal Mitra, B.A., district surveyor, Hamirpur. He has been living with his family in a bungalow for about a year. It is a good small bungalow, with two central and several side rooms. There is a verandah on the south and an enclosure, which serves the purpose of a court-yard for the ladies, on the north. On the eastern side of this enclosure is the kitchen and on the western, the privy. It has a big compound all round, on the south-west corner of

which there is a tomb of some Shahid, known as the tomb of Phulan Shahid.

At about 5 o'clock in the evening on 26th June, 1913, when Mr. Mitra was out in office, it was suddenly noticed that the southern portion of the privy was on fire. People ran for rescue and by their timely assistance it was possible to completely extinguish the fire by means of water which they managed to get at the moment, before the fire could do any real damage. On learning of the fire, the ladies and children, all bewildered, collected in a room, ready to quit the building in case the fire was not checked or took a serious turn. About a square foot of the thatch was burnt. Shortly after this another corner of the house was seen burning. This was in the kitchen. It was not a continuation of the former fire as the latter had been completely extinguished. Not even smoke or a spark was left to kindle. The two places are completely separated from each other being divided by an open court-yard of 30 yards in length and there is no connection between them at all.

There was no fire at the time in the kitchen even, and there were no outsiders besides the ladies and children who were shut up in a room. This too was extinguished without any damage having been done. By this time Mr. Mitra and his several friends turned up on getting the news of the fire in his house. I was one of them. In short the fire broke out in the house at seven different places within an hour or an hour and a half; all these places situated so apart from one another that one was astonished to find how it broke out one after the other without any visible sign of the possibility of a fire from outside. We were all at a loss to account for the breaking out of the fire. To all appearance it broke out each time spontaneously and mysteriously.

The fact that fire broke out so often as seven times within the short space of about an hour and a half, each time at a different place without doing any perceptible damage to the thatching of the bungalow or to any other article of the occupant of the house, is a mystery which remains to be solved. After the last breaking out, it was decided that the house must be vacated at once. Mr. Mitra and his family consequently removed to another house of Padri Ahmad Shah about 200 yards distant therefrom. To the great astonishment of all nothing happened after the 'vacation' of the house for the whole night.

Next morning Mr. Mitra came with his sister to have his morning meals prepared there, thinking that there was no fire during the night. To his great curiosity he found that the house was ablaze within 10 or 15 minutes of his arrival. They removed at once and everything was again all right. A day or two after he removed to a pucca house within the town, not easy to catch fire. After settling his family in the new house Mr. Mitra went to a town (Moudha) some 21 miles from the head quarters. During the night following his departure, a daughter of Mr. Mitra aged about 10 years saw in dream a boy who called himself Shahid Baba. The girl enquired of him about the reason of the fire breaking in her last residence and was told by him that she would witness curious scenes next morning, after which she would be told the remedy. Morning came and it was not long before fire broke out in the second storey of the new house. This was extinguished as easily as the previous ones and it did not cause any damage.

Next came the turn of a dhoti of the girl mentioned above which was hanging in the house. Half of it was completely burnt down before the fire could be extinguished. In succession, the pillow wrapped in a bedding, a sheet of another bedding and lastly the dhoti which the girl was wearing caught fire and were extinguished after they were nearly half destroyed. Mr. Mitra's son aged about 4 months was lying on a cot: as soon as he was lifted up—a portion of the bed on which he was lying was seen burning. Although the pillow was burnt down there was no mark of fire on the bedding. Neither the girl nor the boy received any injury.

Most curious of all, the papers enclosed in

a box were burnt although the box remained closed. B. Ganesh Prasad, munsif, and the post master hearing of this, went to the house and in their presence a mirzai of the girl which was spread over a cot in the court-yard caught fire spontaneously and was seen burning.

Now the girl went to sleep again. It was now about noon. She again saw the same boy in the dream. She was told this time that if the tomb was whitewashed and a promise to repair it within three months made, the trouble would cease. They were also ordained to return to the house which they had left. This command was soon obeyed by the troubled family which removed immediately after the tomb was whitewashed to the bungalow in which they are now peacefully living without the least disturbance or annoyance of any sort. I leave to your readers to draw their own conclusions according to their own experience of life and to form such opinion as they like.

Permeshwar Dayal Amist, B.A.,
July 9. Vakil, High Court

The Examination Paper

This is a story which I believe. Of course, this is not my personal experience; but it has been repeated by so many men, who should have witnessed the incident, with such wonderful accuracy that I cannot but believe it. The thing happened at the Calcutta Medical College.

There was a student who had come from Dacca, the Provincial Capital of Eastern Bengal. Let us call him Jogesh.

Jogesh was a handsome young fellow of about 24. He was a married man and his wife's photograph stood in a frame on his table in the hostel. She was a girl hardly 15 years old and Jogesh was evidently very fond of her. Jogesh used to say a lot of things about his wife's attainments which we (I mean the other students of his class) believed, and a lot more which we did not believe. For instance we believed that she could cook a very good dinner, but that is an ordinary accomplishment of the average Bengali girl of her age.

Jogesh also said that she knew some mystic arts by means of which she could hold communion with him every night. Every morning when he came out of his room he used to say that his wife had been to him during the night and told him—this—that—and the other. This, of course, we did not believe, but as Jogesh was so sensitive we never betrayed our scepticism in his presence. But one significant fact happened one day which rather roused our curiosity.

The Examination Paper

One morning Jogesh came out with a sad expression and told us that his father was ill at home. His wife had informed him at night, he said; at that time we treated the matter with indifference but at about 10 o'clock came a telegram, (which we of course intercepted) intimating that his father was really ill.

The next morning Jogesh charged us with having intercepted his telegram; but we thought that he must have heard about the telegram from one of the students, as there were about half a dozen of us present when the telegram had arrived.

Jogesh's father came round and the matter was forgotten.

Then came the annual University examination.

Jogesh's weak subject was Materia Medica and everybody knew it.

So we suggested that Jogesh should ask his wife what questions would be set, during one of her nightly visits.

After great hesitation Jogesh consented to ask his wife on the night before the examination.

The eventful night came and went. In the morning Jogesh came out and we anxiously inquired what his wife had said.

"She told me the questions" said Jogesh sadly "but she said she would never visit me again here."

The questions were of greater importance and so we wanted to have a look at them. Jogesh had noted these down on the back of a theatre programme (or hand bill—I really forget which) and showed the questions to us. There were eleven of them—all likely questions such as Major—
—might ask. To take the questions down and to learn the answers was the work of an hour, and in spite of our scepticism we did it. And we were glad that we did it.

When the paper was distributed, we found that the questions were identically those which we had seen that very morning and the answers to which we had prepared with so much labour only a few hours before.

The matter came to the notice of the authorities who were all European gentlemen. The eleven answer papers were examined and re-examined, and finally Jogesh was sent for by Col.——the Principal to state how much truth was there in what had been reported, but Jogesh prudently refused to answer the question; and finally the Colonel said that it was all nonsense and that the eleven students knew their Materia Medica very well and that was all. In fact it was the Colonel himself who had taught the subject to his students, and he assured all the eleven students that he was really proud of them. The ten students were however proud of Jogesh and his mystic wife. It was decided that a subscription should be raised and a gold necklace should be presented to Jogesh's wife as a humble token of respect and gratitude of some thankful friends, and this plan was duly executed.

Jogesh is now a full-fledged doctor and so are all the other ten who had got hold of the Materia Medica paper.

After the incident of that night Jogesh's wife had an attack of brain fever and for some time her life was despaired of, and we were all so sorry. But, thank God, she came round after a long and protracted illness, and then we sent her the necklace.

Jogesh told us subsequently that his wife had given him an Indian charm-case with instructions to put it on with a chain round the neck whenever he required her. Immediately he put on the chain, to which this charm-case was attached, round his neck, he felt as if he was in a trance and then his wife came. Whether she came in the flesh or only in spirit Jogesh could not say as he never had the opportunity of touching her so long as she was there, for he could not get up from the bed or the chair or wherever he happened to be. On the last occasion she had entreated him not to press her to tell the questions. He had, however, insisted and so she had dictated to him the examination paper as if from memory. The theatre programme was the only thing within his reach and he had taken down all the questions on that, as he thought he could not rely upon his own memory. Then she had gone away; but before going she had walked up to him, unbuttoned his kurta (native shirt) at the chin, and removed the charm-case from the chain to which it was attached. Then she had vanished and the charm case had vanished too. The chain had, of course, remained on Jogesh's neck. Since that eventful night Jogesh had had no mystic communion with his wife during his stay in Calcutta.

She refused to discuss the subject when Jogesh afterwards met her at Dacca. So the mystery remains unsolved.

The Shakespeare Expert

Talking of questions and answers reminds me of an incident that took place on one occasion in my presence.

A certain Mohammedan hypnotist once visited us when I was at College.

There was a number of us, all students, in the hostel common-room or library when this man came and introduced himself to us as a professional hypnotist. On being asked whether he could show us anything wonderful and convincing he said he could. He asked us to procure a teapoy with 3 strong legs. This we did. Then he asked two of us to sit round that small table and he also sat down. He asked us to put our hands flat on the table and think of some dead person. We thought of a dead friend of ours. After we had thus been seated for about five minutes there was a rap on the leg of the teapoy. We thought that the hypnotist had kicked the leg on his side.

"The spirit has come" said the hypnotist.

"How should we ascertain?" I asked.

"Ask him some question and he will answer" said the hypnotist.

Then we asked how many from our class would obtain the university degree that year.

"Spirit", said the hypnotist "as the names are mentioned one rap means pass, two mean plucked"; then he addressed the others sitting around "see that I am not kicking at the leg of the teapoy."

Half a dozen of the boys sat down on the floor to watch.

As each name was mentioned there came one rap or two raps as the case might be till the whole list was exhausted.

"We can't ascertain the truth of this until 3 months are over" said I.

"How many rupees have I in my pocket" asked one of the lookers-on.

There came three distinct raps and on examining the purse of the person we found that he had exactly 3 rupees and nothing more.

Then we asked a few more questions and the answers came promptly in. "Yes" and "No" by means of raps.

Then according to the hypnotist's suggestion one student wrote a line from Shakespeare and the ghost was asked what that line was.

"As the plays are named rap once at the name of the play from which the passage has been taken" said the hypnotist, solemnly addressing the Spirit.

"Hamlet"
No reply
"King Lear"
No reply
"Merchant of Venice"
No reply
"Macbeth"
One loud rap.
"Macbeth" said the hypnotist "now which Act."
"Act I"
No reply
"Act II"

No reply
"Act III"
No reply
"Act IV"
No reply
"Act V"
One loud rap.
"Scene I"
No reply.
"Scene II"
No reply.
"Scene III"
One loud rap.
"Now what about the lines" said the hypnotist.
"Line one—Two—Three…Thirty nine"
No reply.
"Forty"
One loud rap
"Forty one"
One loud rap
"Forty two"
One loud rap
"Forty three"
One loud rap
"Forty four"
One loud rap
"Forty five"
One loud rap
"Forty six"
No reply

A copy of Shakespeare's Macbeth was at once procured and opened at Act V, Sec. III, line 40.

"Can'st thou not minister to a mind diseased, Pluck from the memory a rooted sorrow, Raze out the written troubles of the brain, And with some sweet oblivious antidote, Cleanse the stuff'd bosom of that perilous stuff, Which weighs upon the heart?"

This was what we read.

The student was then asked to produce his paper and on it was the identical quotation.

Then the hypnotist asked us to remove our hands from the top of the teapoy. The hypnotist did the same thing and said "The Spirit has gone."

We all stared at each other in mute surprise.

Afterwards we organized a big show for the benefit of the hypnotist, and that was a grand success.

Lots of strange phenomena were shown to us which are too numerous to mention. The fellows who had sat on the floor watching whether or not it was the hypnotist who was kicking at the teapoy-leg assured us that he was not.

The strange feats of this man, (hypnotist astrologer and thought-reader all rolled into one) have ever since remained an insoluble mystery.

The Messenger of Death

We have often been told how some of us receive in an unlooked-for manner an intimation of death some time before that incident does actually occur.

The late Mr. W. T. Stead, before he sailed for America in the Titanic had made his will and given his friends clearly to understand that he would see England no more.

Others have also had such occult premonitions, so to say, a few days, and sometimes weeks, before their death.

We also know a number of cases in which people have received similar intimation of the approaching death of a near relation or a dear friend who, in most cases, lives at a distance.

There is a well-known family in England (one of the peers of the realm) in whose case previous intimation of death comes in a peculiar form. Generally when the family is at dinner a carriage is heard to drive up to the portico. Everybody thinks it is some absent guest who has arrived late and my lord or my lady gets up to see who it is. Then when the hall door is opened it is seen that there is no carriage at all. This is a sure indication of an impending death in the family.

I know another very peculiar instance. A certain gentleman in Bengal died leaving four sons and a widow. The youngest was about 5 years old. These children used to live with their mother in the family residence under the guardianship of their uncle.

One night the widow had a peculiar dream. It seemed to her that her husband had returned from a long journey for an hour or so and was going away again. Of course, in her dream the lady forgot all about her widowhood.

Before his departure the husband proposed that she should allow him to take one of the sons with him and she might keep the rest.

The widow readily agreed and it was settled that the youngest but one should go with the husband. The boy was called, and he very willingly agreed to go with his father. The mother gave him a last hug and kiss and passed him on to the father who carried him away.

The next moment the widow woke. She remembered every particular of the dream. A cold sweat stood on her forehead when she comprehended what she had done.

The boy died the next morning. When she told me the story she said that the only consolation that she had was that the child was safe with his father. A very poor consolation indeed!

Now this is a peculiar story told in a peculiar fashion; but I know one or two wonderful stories which are more peculiar still.

Goats

> India's religious rites and customs, familiar to many readers, can also bring about strange events......

It is a custom in certain families in Bengal that in connection with the Durga pooja black-male goats are offered as a sacrifice. In certain other families strictly vegetarian offerings are made.

The mode of sacrificing the goat is well known to some readers, and will not interest those who do not know the custom. The fact remains that millions of goats are sacrificed all over Bengal during the three days of the Durga pooja and on the Shyama pooja night, (i.e. Diwali or Dipavali).

There is however nothing ominous in all this, except when the "sacrificial sword" fails to sever the head of the goat from the trunk at one deadly stroke. As this bodes ill the householder to appease the deity, to whose wrath such failure is imputed, sacrifices another goat then and there and further offers to do penance by sacrificing double the number of goats next year.

But what is more pertinent to the subject I am dealing with is the sacrificing of goats under peculiar circumstances. Thus when an epidemic (such as cholera, small pox and now probably plague) breaks out in a village in Bengal all the principal residents of the place in order to propitiate the deity to whose curse or ire the visitation is supposed to be due, raise a sufficient amount by subscription for worshipping the irate Goddess.

The black he-goat that is offered as a sacrifice on such an occasion is not actually slain, but being besmeared with "Sindur" (red oxide of mercury) and generally having one of the ears cropped or bored is let loose, i.e. allowed to roam about until clandestinely passed on to some neighbouring village to which, the goat is credited with the virtue of transferring the epidemic from the village originally infected.

The goats thus marked are not looked upon with particular favour in the villages. They are generally not ill-treated by the villagers, and when they eat up the cabbages, etc. all that the poor villagers can do is to curse them and drive them away—but they return as soon as the poor owner of the garden has moved away. Such goats become, in consequence, very bold and give a lot of trouble.

When, therefore, such a billy-goat appears in a village what the villagers generally do is to hire a boat, carry the goat a long distance along the river, say 20 or 25 miles and leave him there. Now the villagers of the place where such a goat is left play the same trick, so it sometimes happens that the goat comes back after a week or so.

Once it so happened that a dedicated goat made his unwelcome appearance in a certain village in Bengal.

The villagers hired a boat and carried him about 20 miles up the river and left him there. The goat came back after a week. Then they left him at a place 20 miles down the river and he came back again. Afterwards they took the goat 50 miles up and down the river but each time the goat returned like the proverbial bad penny.

After trying all kinds of tricks in their attempt to get rid of the goat the villagers became desperate. So a few hot-headed young men of the village in an evil hour decided to kill the goat. Instead of killing the goat quietly (as probably they should have done) and throwing the body into the river, they organised a grand feast and ate the flesh of the dedicated goat.

Within 24 hours of the dinner each one of them who had taken part in it was attacked with cholera of a most virulent type and within another 24 hours every one of them was dead. Medical and scientific experts were called in from Calcutta to explain the cause of the calamity, but no definite results were obtained from these investigations. One thing, however, was certain. There was no poison of any kind in the food.

The cause of the death of about 30 young men remains a mystery.

This was retribution with a vengeance and the writer does not see the justice of the divine providence in this particular case.

The Messenger of Death II

> The coming of the messenger of death is manifest in many ways......

In another village the visit of the messenger of death was also marked in a peculiar fashion.

Two men one tall and the other short, the tall man carrying a lantern, are seen to enter the house of one of the villagers; and the next morning there is a death in the house which they entered.

When, for the first time, these two mysterious individuals were seen to enter a house an alarm of thieves was raised. The house was searched but no trace of any stranger was found in the house. The poor villager who had given the alarm was publicly scolded for his folly after the fruitless search, for thinking that thieves would come with a lighted lantern. But that poor man had mentioned the lighted lantern before the search commenced and nobody had thought that fact "absurd" at that time.

Since that date a number of people has seen these messengers of death enter the houses of several persons, and whenever they enter a house a death takes place in that house within the next 24 hours.

Some of the witnesses who have seen these messengers of death are too cautious and too respectable to be disbelieved or doubted. Your humble servant on one occasion passed a long time in this village, but he, fortunately or unfortunately, call it what you please, never saw these fell messengers of death.

In another family in Bengal death of a member is foretold a couple of days before the event in a very peculiar manner.

This is a very rich family having a large residential house with a private temple or chapel attached to it, but the members never pay a penny to the doctor or the chemist either.

In many rich families in Bengal there are private deities the worship of which is conducted by the heads of the families assisted by the family priests. There are generally private temples adjoining the houses or rooms set apart for such idols, and all the members of the family and especially the ladies say their prayers there.

Such a temple remains open during the day and is kept securely closed at night, because nobody should be allowed to disturb the deity at night and also because there is generally a lot of gold and silver articles in the temple which an unorthodox thief may carry away.

Now what I have just mentioned was the custom of the particular house-hold referred to above.

One night a peculiar groan was heard issuing from the temple. All the inmates of the house came to see what the matter was. The key of the temple was with the family priest who was not present. He had probably gone to some other person's house to have a smoke and a chat, and it was an hour before the key could be procured and the door of the temple opened.

Everything was just as it had been left 3 or 4 hours previously. The cause or origin of the groans was never traced or discovered.

The next morning one of the members of the family was suddenly taken ill and died before medical aid could be obtained from Calcutta.

This was about fifty years ago. Since then the members of this family have become rather accustomed to these groans.

If there is a case of real Asiatic cholera or a case of double pneumonia they don't call in a doctor though there is a very capable and learned medical man within a mile.

But if once the groans are heard the person, who gets the smallest pin-prick the next morning, dies; and no medical science has ever done any good.

"The most terrible thing in this connection is the suspense" said one of the members of that family to me once. "As a rule you hear the groans at night and then you have to wait till the morning to ascertain whose turn it is. Generally however you find long before sunrise that somebody has become very ill. If not, you have to wire to all the absent members of the family in the morning to enquire—what you can guess. And you have to await the replies to the telegrams. How the minutes pass between the hearing of the groans till it is actually ascertained who is going to die—need not be described."

"You must have been having an exciting time of it" I asked this young man.

"Generally not, because we find that somebody is ill from before and then we know what is going to happen" said my informant.

"But during your experience of 25 years you must have been very nervous about these groans yourself at times," I asked.

"On two occasions only we had to be nervous because nobody was ill beforehand; but in each case that person died who was the most afraid. I was not nervous on these occasions myself, for some reason or other."

These uncanny groans of the messenger of death have remained a mystery for the last fifty years.

I know another family in which the death of the head of the family is predicted in a very peculiar manner.

There is a big picture of the Goddess Kali in the family. On the night of the Shyama pooja (Dewali) which occurs about the middle of November, this picture is brought out and worshipped.

The picture is a big oil painting of the old Indian School and has a massive solid gold frame. The picture is a beauty—a thing worth seeing.

All the year round it hangs on the eastern wall of the room occupied by the head of the family.

Now the peculiar thing with this family is that no male member of the family dies out of his turn. The eldest male member dies leaving behind everybody else. The next man then becomes the eldest and dies afterwards and so on.

But before the death of the head of the family the warning comes in a peculiar way.

The picture of the goddess is found hanging upside down. One morning when the head of the family comes out of his bed-room and the youngsters go in to make the room tidy, as they call it, (though they generally make the room more untidy and finally leave it to the servants) they find the famous family picture hanging literally topsyturvy (that is with head downwards) and they at once sound the alarm. Then they all know that the head of the family is doomed and will die within a week.

But this fact does not disturb the normal quiet of the family. Because the pater familias is generally very old and infirm and more generally quite prepared to die.

But the fact remains that so long as the warning does not come in this peculiar fashion every member of the household knows that there is no immediate danger.

For instance it is only when this warning comes that all the children who are out of the station are wired for.

Every reader must admit that this is rather weird.

From the Desk of
S. Mukerji Esq.,
Ghost Story Collector Extraordinary
Allahabad

July 1917

Dear Honoured and Esteemed Reader

Since the publication of the first edition my attention has been drawn to a number of very interesting and instructive articles that have been appearing in the papers from time to time. Readers who care for subjects like the present must have themselves noted these; but there is one article which, by reason of the great interest created in the German Kaiser at the present moment, I am forced to reproduce. As permission to reproduce the article was delayed the book was through the press by the time it arrived. I am therefore reproducing on the following pages the article as it appeared in *The Occult Review* of January 1917. My grateful thanks are due to the proprietors and the Editor of *The Occult Review* but for whose kind permission some of my readers would have been deprived of a most interesting treat.

S. Mukerji

The White Lady of the Hohenzollerns

A great deal has been written and said concerning the various appearances of the famous White Lady of the Hohenzollerns. As long ago as the fifteenth century she was seen, for the first time, in the old Castle of Neuhaus, in Bohemia, looking out at noon day from an upper window of an uninhabited turret of the castle, and numerous indeed are the stories of her appearances to various persons connected with the Royal House of Prussia, from that first one in the turret window down to the time of the death of the late Empress Augusta, which was, of course, of comparatively recent date. For some time after that event, she seems to have taken a rest; and now, if rumour is to be credited, the apparition which displayed in the past so deep an interest in the fortunes—or perhaps one would be more correct in saying misfortunes—of the Hohenzollern family has been manifesting herself again!

The remarkable occurrences of which I am about to write were related by certain French persons of sound sense and unimpeachable veracity, who happened to be in Berlin a few weeks before the outbreak of the European War. The Kaiser, the most superstitious monarch who ever sat upon the Prussian throne, sternly forbade the circulation of the report of these happenings in his own country, but our gallant Allies across the Channel are, fortunately, not obliged to obey the despotic commands of Wilhelm II, and these persons, therefore, upon their return to France, related, to those interested in such matters, the following story of the great War Lord's three visitations from the dreaded ghost of the Hohenzollerns.

Early in the summer of 1914 it was rumoured, in Berlin, that the White Lady had made her re-appearance. The tale, whispered first of all at Court, spread, gradually amongst the townspeople. The Court, alarmed, tried to suppress it, but it refused to be suppressed, and eventually there was scarcely a man, woman or child in the neighbourhood who did not say—irrespective of whether they believed it or not—that the White Lady, the shadowy spectre whose appearance always foreboded disaster to the Imperial House, had been recently seen, not once, but three times, and by no less a person than Kaiser Wilhelm himself!

The first of these appearances, so rumour stated, took place one night at the end of June. The hour was late: the Court, which was then in residence at the palace of Potsdam, was wrapped in slumber; all was quiet. There was an almost death-like silence in the palace. In one wing were the apartments of the Empress, where she lay sleeping; in the opposite wing slept one of her sons; the other Princes were in Berlin. In an entirely different part of the royal residence, guarded by three sentinels in a spacious antechamber, sat the Emperor in his private study. He had been lately, greatly engrossed in weighty matters of State, and for some time past it had been his habit to work thus, far into the night. That same evening the Chancellor, von Bethman-Hollweg, had had a private audience of his Majesty, and had left the royal presence precisely at 11-30, carrying an enormous dossier under his arm. The Emperor had accompanied him as far as the door, shaken hands with him, then returned to his work at his writing-desk.

Midnight struck, and still the Emperor, without making the slightest sound, sat on within the room. The guards without began to grow slightly uneasy, for at midnight punctually—not a minute before, not a minute after—it was the Emperor's unfailing custom, when he was working late at night, to ring and order a light repast to be brought to him. Sometimes it used to be a cup of thick chocolate, with hot cakes; sometimes a few sandwiches of smoked ham with a glass of Munich or Pilsen beer—but, as this particular midnight hour struck the guards awaited the royal commands in vain. The Emperor had apparently forgotten to order his midnight meal!

One o'clock in the morning came, and still the Emperor's bell had not sounded. Within the study silence continued to reign—silence as profound indeed as that of the grave. The uneasiness of the three guards without increased; they glanced at each other with anxious faces. Was their royal master taken ill? All during the day he had seemed to be labouring under the influence of some strange, suppressed excitement, and as he had bidden good-bye to the Chancellor they had noticed that the expression of excitement on his face had increased. That something of grave import was in the air they, and indeed every one surrounding the Emperor, had long been aware, it was just possible that the strain of State affairs was becoming too much for him, and that he had been smitten with sudden indisposition. And yet, after all, he had probably only fallen asleep! Whichever it was, however, they were uncertain how to act. If they thrust ceremony aside and entered the study, they knew that very likely they would only expose themselves to the royal anger. The order was strict, "When the Emperor works in his study no one may enter it without being bidden." Should they inform the Lord Chamberlain of the palace? But, if there was no sufficiently serious reason for such a step, they would incur his anger, almost as terrible to face as that of their royal master.

A little more time dragged by, and at last, deciding to risk the consequences, the guards approached the study. One of them, the most courageous of the three, lifted a heavy curtain, and slowly and cautiously opened the door. He gave one rapid glance into the room beyond, then, returning to his companions said in a low voice and with a terrified gesture towards the interior of the study:

"Look!"

The two guards obeyed him, and an alarming spectacle met their eyes. In the middle of the room, beside a big table littered with papers and military documents, lay the Emperor, stretched full length upon the thick velvet pile carpet, one hand, as if to hide something dreadful from view, across his face. He was quite unconscious, and while two of the guards endeavoured to revive him, the other ran for the doctor. Upon the doctor's arrival they carried him to his sleeping apartments, and after some time succeeded in reviving him. The Emperor then, in trembling accents, told his astounded listeners what had occurred.

Exactly at midnight, according to his custom, he had rung the bell which was the signal that he was ready for his repast. Curiously enough, neither of the guards, although they had been listening for it, had heard that bell.

He had rung quite mechanically, and also mechanically, had turned again to his writing desk directly he had done so. A few minutes later he had heard the door open and footsteps approach him across the soft carpet. Without raising his head from his work he had commenced to say:

"Bring me—"

Then he had raised his head, expecting to see the butler awaiting his orders. Instead his eyes fell upon a shadowy female figure dressed in white, with a long, flowing black veil trailing behind her on the ground. He rose from his chair, terrified, and cried:

"Who are you, and what do you want?"

At the same moment, instinctively, he placed his hand upon a service revolver which lay upon the desk. The white figure, however, did not move, and he advanced towards her. She gazed at him, retreating slowly backwards towards the end of the room, and finally disappeared through the door which gave access to the antechamber without. The door, however, had not opened, and the three guards stationed in the antechamber, as has been already stated, had neither seen nor heard anything of the apparition. At the moment of her disappearance the Emperor fell into a swoon, remaining in that condition until the guards and the doctor revived him.

Such was the story, gaining ground every day in Berlin, of the first of the three appearances of the White Lady of the Hohenzollerns to the Kaiser. The story of her second appearance to him, which occurred some two or three weeks later, is equally remarkable.

On this occasion she did not visit him at Potsdam, but at Berlin, and instead of the witching hour of midnight, she chose the broad, clear light of day. Indeed, during the whole of her career, the White Lady does not seem to have kept to the time-honoured traditions of most ghosts, and appeared to startled humanity chiefly at night time or in dim uncertain lights. She has never been afraid to face the honest daylight, and that, in my opinion, has always been a great factor in establishing her claim to genuineness. A ghost who is seen by sane people, in full daylight, cannot surely be a mere legendary myth!

It was an afternoon of bright summer—that fateful summer whose blue skies were so soon to be darkened by the sinister clouds of war! The Royal Standard, intimating to the worthy citizens of Berlin the presence of their Emperor, floated gaily over the Imperial residence in the gentle breeze. The Emperor, wrapped in heavy thought—there was much for the mighty War Lord to think about during those last pregnant days before plunging Europe into an agony of tears and blood!—was pacing, alone, up and down a long gallery within the palace.

His walk was agitated; there was a troubled frown upon his austere countenance. Every now and then he paused in his walk, and withdrew from his pocket a piece of paper, which he carefully read and re-read, and as he did so, angry, muttered words broke from him, and his hand flew instinctively to his sword hilt. Occasionally he raised his eyes to the walls on either side of him, upon which hung numerous portraits of his distinguished ancestors. He studied them gravely, from Frederick I, Burgrave of Nuremburg, to that other Frederick, his own father, and husband of the fair English princess against whose country he was so shortly going to wage the most horrible warfare that has ever been waged in the whole history of the world!

Suddenly, from the other end of the long portrait gallery he perceived coming towards him a shadowy female figure, dressed entirely in white, and carrying a large bunch of keys in her hand. She was not, this time, wearing the long flowing black veil in which she had appeared to him a few weeks previously, but the Emperor instantly recognized her, and the blood froze in his veins. He stood rooted to the ground, unable to advance or to retreat, paralysed with horror, the hair rising on his head, beads of perspiration standing on his brow.

The figure continued to advance in his direction, slowly, noiselessly, appearing rather to glide than to walk over the floor. There was an expression of the deepest sadness upon her countenance, and as she drew near to the stricken man watching her, she held out her arms towards him, as if to enfold him. The Emperor, his horror increasing, made a violent effort to move, but in vain. He seemed indeed paralysed; his limbs, his muscles, refused to obey him.

Then suddenly, just as the apparition came close up to him and he felt, as on the former occasion when he had been visited by her, that he was going to faint, she turned abruptly and moved away in the direction of a small side door. This she opened with her uncanny bunch of keys and without turning her head, disappeared.

At the exact moment of her disappearance the Emperor recovered his faculties. He was able to move, he was able to speak; his arms, legs, tongue, obeyed his autocratic will once more. He uttered a loud terrified cry, which resounded throughout the palace. Officers, chamberlains, guards, servants, came running to the gallery, white-faced, to see what had happened. They found their royal master in a state bordering on collapse. Yet, to the anxious questions which they put to him, he only replied incoherently and evasively; it was as if he knew something terrible, something dreadful, but did not wish to speak of it. Eventually he retired to his own apartments, but it was not until several hours had passed that he returned to his normal condition of mind.

The same doctor who had been summoned on the occasion of Wilhelm's former encounter with the White Lady was in attendance on him, and he looked extremely grave when informed that the Emperor had again experienced a mysterious shock. He shut himself up alone with his royal patient, forbidding any one else access to the private apartments. However, in spite of all precautions, the story of what had really occurred in the picture gallery eventually leaked out—it is said through a maid of honour, who heard it from the Empress.

The third appearance of the White Lady of the Hohenzollerns to the Kaiser did not take place at either of the palaces, but strangely enough, in a forest, though exactly where situated has not been satisfactorily verified.

In the middle of the month of July, 1914, while the war-clouds were darkening every hour, the Emperor's movements were very unsettled. He was constantly travelling from place to place, and one day—so it was afterwards said in Berlin—while on a hunting expedition, he suddenly encountered a phantom female figure, dressed in white, who, springing apparently from nowhere, stopped in front of his horse, and blew a shadowy horn, frightening the animal so much that its rider was nearly thrown to the ground. The phantom figure then disappeared, as mysteriously as it had come—but that it was the White Lady of the Hohenzollerns, come, perchance, to warn Wilhelm of some terrible future fate, there was little doubt in the minds of those who afterwards heard of the occurrence.

According to one version of the story of this third appearance, the phantom was also seen by two officers who were riding by the Emperor's side, but the general belief is that she manifested herself, as on the two former occasions, to Wilhelm alone.

There are many who will not believe in the story, no doubt, and there are also many who will. For my own part, I am inclined to think that, if the ghost of the Hohenzollerns was able to manifest herself so often on the eve of any tragedy befalling them in past, it would be strange indeed if she had not manifested herself on the eve of this greatest tragedy of all—the War!

CLASSIC SF FROM LEONAUR
AVAILABLE IN SOFTCOVER OR HARDCOVER WITH DUST JACKET

SF1 CLASSIC SCIENCE FICTION SERIES
BEFORE ADAM & Other Stories
by Jack London

Volume 1 of The Collected Science Fiction & Fantasy of Jack London.
SOFTCOVER : **ISBN 1-84677-008-4**
HARDCOVER : **ISBN 1-84677-015-7**

Contains the complete novel Before Adam plus shorter works: The Scarlet Plague, A Relic of the Pliocene, When the World Was Young, The Red One, Planchette, A Thousand Deaths, Goliah, A Curious Fragment and The Rejuvenation of Major Rathbone

SF2 CLASSIC SCIENCE FICTION SERIES
THE IRON HEEL & Other Stories
by Jack London

Volume 2 of The Collected Science Fiction & Fantasy of Jack London.
SOFTCOVER : **ISBN 1-84677-004-1**
HARDCOVER : **ISBN 1-84677-011-4**

Contains the complete novel The Iron Heel plus shorter works: The Enemy of All the World, The Shadow and the Flash, The Strength of the Strong, The Unparalleled Invasion and The Dream of Debs

SF3 CLASSIC SCIENCE FICTION SERIES
THE STAR ROVER & Other Stories
by Jack London

Volume 3 of The Collected Science Fiction & Fantasy of Jack London.
SOFTCOVER : **ISBN 1-84677-006-8**
HARDCOVER : **ISBN 1-84677-013-0**

Contains the complete novel The Star Rover plus shorter works: The Minions of Midas, The Eternity of Forms and The Man With the Gash

AVAILABLE ONLINE AT
www.leonaur.com
AND OTHER GOOD BOOK STORES

CLASSIC SF FROM LEONAUR
AVAILABLE IN SOFTCOVER OR HARDCOVER WITH DUST JACKET

SF4 CLASSIC SCIENCE FICTION SERIES
DARKNESS & DAWN 1: The Vacant World
by George Allen England

SOFTCOVER : ISBN 1-84677-027-0
HARDCOVER : ISBN 1-84677-034-3

New York City – the end of the 3rd millennium. Buildings in ruins. Central Park a jungle peopled by sub-humans. A huge black shape moving across the night sky. Civilization has vanished along with humankind. Into this hostile new world two survivors of our enlightened age awaken from 1000 years of slumber - to fall victims to a world gone wild? - or to give mankind a second chance?

SF5 CLASSIC SCIENCE FICTION SERIES
DARKNESS & DAWN 2: Beyond the Great Oblivion
by George Allen England

SOFTCOVER : ISBN 1-84677-028-9
HARDCOVER : ISBN 1-84677-036-X

The distant future - exotic flora and fauna thrive - savage tribes of cannibalistic sub-humans fight for dominance. New York is a place of little hope! The last vestiges of humanity set out across America's devastated landscape in search of their dream, enticed onward by a mysterious and vast black chasm 500 miles deep - does the future threaten extinction for mankind? - or offer one last chance of redemption?

SF6 CLASSIC SCIENCE FICTION SERIES
DARKNESS & DAWN 3: The After Glow
by George Allen England

SOFTCOVER : ISBN 1-84677-029-7
HARDCOVER : ISBN 1-84677-038-6

Near the Great Lakes, 1000 years from now. Below our planet's surface tribes of albino warriors eke out an existence in a hostile environment. They tell stories of a golden age; but such tales are mere myths - until a man and a woman with god-like abilities arrive and promise to lead them towards the surface, towards the light and to a new life of plenty.

AVAILABLE ONLINE AT
www.leonaur.com
AND OTHER GOOD BOOK STORES

ALSO FROM LEONAUR
AVAILABLE IN SOFTCOVER OR HARDCOVER WITH DUST JACKET

EW2 EYEWITNESS TO WAR SERIES
CAPTAIN OF THE 95th (Rifles) by Jonathan Leach

An officer of Wellington's Sharpshooters during the Peninsular, South of France and Waterloo Campaigns of the Napoleonic Wars.

SOFTCOVER : ISBN 1-84677-001-7
HARDCOVER : ISBN 1-84677-016-5

WF1 THE WARFARE FICTION SERIES
NAPOLEONIC WAR STORIES
by Sir Arthur Quiller-Couch

Tales of soldiers, spies, battles & Sieges from the Peninsular & Waterloo campaigns

SOFTCOVER : ISBN 1-84677-003-3
HARDCOVER : ISBN 1-84677-014-9

EW1 EYEWITNESS TO WAR SERIES
RIFLEMAN COSTELLO by Edward Costello

The adventures of a soldier of the 95th (Rifles) in the Peninsular & Waterloo Campaigns of the Napoleonic wars.

SOFTCOVER : ISBN 1-84677-000-9
HARDCOVER : ISBN 1-84677-018-1

MC1 THE MILITARY COMMANDERS SERIES
JOURNALS OF ROBERT ROGERS OF THE RANGERS by Robert Rogers

The exploits of Rogers & the Rangers in his own words during 1755-1761 in the French & Indian War.

SOFTCOVER : ISBN 1-84677-002-5
HARDCOVER : ISBN 1-84677-010-6

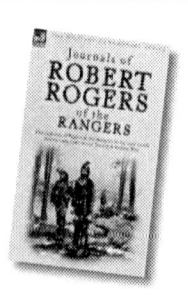

AVAILABLE ONLINE AT
www.leonaur.com
AND OTHER GOOD BOOK STORES